Son of an Arizona Legend

Also by Stephen Bly
in Large Print:

Hard Winter at Broken Arrow Crossing
False Claims at the Little Stephen Mine
Last Hanging at Paradise Meadow
Standoff at Sunrise Creek
Final Justice at Adobe Wells
The Lost Manuscript of
  Martin Taylor Harrison

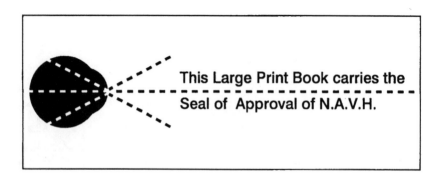

Son of an Arizona Legend

Stephen Bly

G.K. Hall & Co.
Thorndike, Maine

Published in 1996 by arrangement with Crossway Books,
a division of Good News Publishers.

G.K. Hall Large Print Western Collection.

The text of this Large Print edition is unabridged.
Other aspects of the book may vary from the original edition.

Set in 16 pt. Century Schoolbook by Al Chase.

Printed in the United States on permanent paper.

Library of Congress Cataloging in Publication Data

Bly, Stephen A., 1944–
    Son of an Arizona legend / Stephen Bly.
      p.   cm.
    ISBN 0-7838-1783-5 (lg. print : hc)
    1. Large type books. I. Title.
    [PS3552.L93S6 1996]
    813'.54—dc20   96-10458

For
Ted B.
after 83 years
still ridin' tall

ONE

September 17, 1888,
eastern Yavapai County,
Arizona Territory.

The hot blast of westerly wind bore no hint of autumn, let alone winter. Stuart Brannon could hear the dry grass grind beneath every step of his big black horse, Dos Vientos. He nudged the animal higher up the mountain slope along Sunrise Creek.

In the springtime, the creek roared off the Mazatzal Mountains and tumbled with vibrant, refreshing purity into the holding ponds at the Triple-B Ranch. In the springtime, a cowboy was lucky to cross the twenty-foot-wide creek at any point. In the springtime, the wildflowers lined the banks, the cottonwoods leafed fervent green, and the grass promised abundant feed. But this was not springtime.

Brannon glanced again at the stream, no more than two or three feet wide. It hardly flowed, but seeped from stagnant pool to stagnant pool, somehow easing itself down the mountainside like an old man descending a stairway.

The cottonwoods still clung to life . . . but listlessly, like besieged sentinels waiting to be

7

rescued. It had been so long since the grass was green that the hillside seemed permanently brown.

"Well, it's as dry as a promise in a frying pan," Brannon announced to the black horse as he dismounted. He loosed the cincha, dropped the reins to the ground, and allowed the horse to find a drink on his own.

Sinking to his knees near a pond of clear water no bigger than a couple of wash basins, Brannon shoved his black hat, crown down, into a leafless bush and leaned over the pool.

The sun was still high, and the reflection in the water was clear. He could see his white forehead above the hat line and his tough, brown face below that line. Crowfeet and deep wrinkles surrounded his eyes like wolves circling for a kill. Gray was the dominant color of hair both at the temples and hanging over his ears.

I look more like my granddad every day!

A one-inch streak of dried blood branded his neck — a trophy of a hurried shaving job early that morning. There was some sort of dirt smudge above his left eye, making his eyebrow look permanently raised. His lips, as always, were chapped.

Unbuttoning the sleeves on his gray cotton shirt, he rolled them up to his elbows. Then he loosened his red bandanna and plunged it into the water. Wringing it out, he washed his neck.

The water felt warm — almost hot — as it ran

down his neck and chest on the inside of his shirt. He scrubbed his face clean, rinsed out the bandanna, and retied it around his neck.

Brannon, you look like a saddle bum ridin' the high line. And if we don't get some fall rain . . . You just might be doin' that.

He leaned back against the trunk of a broken cottonwood and cautiously tugged at his right boot. The fifteen-inch shaft held his foot tight, and he glanced around for a forked branch to use as a boot jack. Finding none, he once again tugged on the boot until it slipped out of his ducking trousers and off his foot. With great care he unwrapped the linen strip around his large toe and surveyed the damage.

It's broken. There's no doubt about that! I've got to figure out some kind of splint to tie that thing down, or it will permanently stick out like a ripe plum.

At least I should have a good story to tell . . . about taking a shot from an outlaw . . . or being trampled by a stampeding bull . . . or rescuing a maiden from a runaway stage.

He sighed and carefully rubbed his toe.

You're gettin' old, Stuart Brannon.

Easing the throbbing foot into the water, he reached for his hat. Then he lay on his back on the dry grass along the creek, placing the hat, not over his face, but rather on his belt buckle. Then he closed his eyes and relaxed.

The sun blazed his face into a full sweat.

Lord, You said in Your Book that You 'sendeth

rain on the just and on the unjust.' Well, I figure that both of us are pretty well needin' it about now. It would be a mighty fine birthday present . . . yep, a mighty fine birthday present.

His mind flashed to his last birthday, and his good friends and neighbors came to mind.

Now I suppose Earl, Julie, and the kids will drop by today with a cake. I swear, she treats me like I was her father . . . fussin' around with the house and remindin' me of —

"And here we have El Brannon! When he was a young man, he was greatly to be feared!" a voice shouted from behind the trees.

Brannon's eyes shot open, but he didn't move. The voice was familiar. Without even looking back, he called out, "Cerdo! You should have more respect for a sleeping old man!" He kept both hands under his hat.

The young Apache rode a paint horse near the reclining Brannon. Another Indian, riding a gray pony, stayed behind the trees.

"You are fortunate I came as a friend," the Indian laughed as he slid down off the paint. "Or I would have had your old gray scalp for sure."

"You are fortunate I recognized it was you," Brannon replied, pulling his hat away from his belt, revealing his Colt .44 positioned in his right hand.

"El Brannon always sleeps with a cocked revolver?"

10

"Yep. Now what are you two doing down here?" Brannon stood up, revealing his bootless foot. He noticed that Cerdo was now as tall as he was.

"We came to see you," the Apache reported.

"About what?"

"There is no water left in the tanks on the mountain. We want to use some from your pond."

"Up at the springs?"

"Yes."

"Sure . . . help yourselves . . . but there's not much left, you know."

"Yes, we would not have asked anyone else. We would have just taken the water, but Cholla insisted that we will ask our friend, El Brannon."

"How is your grandfather?" Brannon asked.

"Old, tired, and discouraged."

Brannon stared at Cerdo for a few minutes, remembering his Apache friends.

"Well, tell Cholla he is always welcome to the water at the springs . . . and he is welcome at the Triple-B."

The Indian behind the trees called out to Cerdo in Apache.

"He asks, 'What happened to El Brannon's foot?' "

"Tell him I broke my toe."

Cerdo repeated the message, then nodded, and laughed at the next question.

"He says, 'I know the toe is broken. Anyone

could see that. But I do not know how El Brannon broke it.' "

"I don't want to talk about it!" Brannon huffed.

Cerdo laughed and climbed back on his paint horse. Then looking at the distant western horizon, he pointed. "Well," he added, "maybe you want to talk about the fire!"

"Fire?"

"In the valley next to your ranch. Yet the wind drifts this way."

Brannon let out a groan as he crammed his foot back into his boot and quickly climbed aboard Dos Vientos.

"It looks like maybe a building," Cerdo advised. "A grass fire would spread more quickly and would not be so thick."

"There's no one living in that valley. The Howlands are on the old Quilici ranch, and then . . . the church! Not the church!"

Brannon jerked the horse around to the west.

"We would go and help El Brannon," Cerdo explained, "but if Apaches are spotted off the reservation, they will be blamed for setting the fire in the first place."

"Hasta luego, amigo," Brannon called.

"Yes, yes." Cerdo nodded. "Until later."

Sunrise Creek Community Church had been built a few years earlier by Brannon and the Quilicis. It served the spiritual needs of most of the residents of eastern Yavapai County. Preachers came out from Prescott and other towns, as available. The rest of the time Brannon and the others filled in.

Lord . . . not the church! It's about the only civilizing thing we have in this whole country!

Dos Vientos felt rested beneath him, and Brannon pushed the horse to a fast trot down the mountain slope. It was way too distant to gallop, but he refused to let the horse back off. After an hour of tough riding, Brannon crested the final hill and could look down the valley at the church in the distance. Billowing clouds of white smoke roared skyward on the far side of the building.

"There's no water!" he moaned. "The spring at the church has been dry for weeks!"

The smoke seemed contained on the far side of the log building. Brannon couldn't spot any damage to the structure itself.

"Maybe it's just starting. No, it's been burning over an hour. Maybe Earl's been here and put the worst of it out. Or maybe . . . Lord, not the church!"

He circled the single-room building that stood among scattered short pines and came face to face with a blazing fire in the cord wood stacked neatly in the yard.

A woodpile fire? But how in the world?

Brannon yanked off his blanket tied to the cantle of his saddle, leaped off the horse, and ran toward the fire. As he did, he smashed his right boot into a half-buried rock, and the pain from his broken toe shot through his leg. He collapsed in the dirt beside the fire.

Instantly he felt the hard steel of a rifle barrel pressed against the back of his neck.

"You made this awful easy, Brannon . . . awful easy!" a voice snarled. "Don't even think about reachin' for that Colt!"

For Brannon, it was a voice from somewhere in the past . . . perhaps the voice of a desperate man. The yet-unseen gunman reached down and lifted Brannon's revolver from its holster.

"Now turn over," the man commanded, "but don't try to get up. You understand?"

"Yeah," Brannon groaned. Then, as the rifle barrel receded, he rolled to his back.

Standing above him and a few feet to the right was a tall, thin man with dark hair, broad shoulders, and a Winchester '73 with long-range peep sight.

"Andrews?" Brannon choked as the smoke from the fire billowed around him. "Tap Andrews?"

"Now isn't that nice — the sheriff remembers me!" the man barked.

"I was never the sheriff," Brannon informed him.

"Brannon, you've always been a sheriff no matter where you were. You're the one who brought me in."

Brannon sat up but made no move toward the gunman. "You escaped from jail. You had to stand trial."

"I escaped because I wouldn't get a fair trial

14

in Globe City. You knew that when you hauled me in."

"Look, Andrews, I told you seven years ago you needed to stand trial and prove your innocence. Trying to escape didn't help your case."

"Ten years at Yuma, that's what they gave me, Brannon. Now that's a pretty steep sentence for a man who never killed that banker."

"Tap, I heard you broke out of A.T.P. years ago. Last I heard you were up in Wyoming or the Dakotas or somewhere."

"Oh, I escaped, all right, but that don't mean the score is settled."

"Well," Brannon sighed, "I don't suppose this means much . . . but I'm glad you got out of Yuma; it was a bum trial and everyone knew it."

"No thanks to you, Brannon. I didn't see you help bust me out."

"Nope, I didn't. So I figure you're still mighty bitter. But that kind of feelin' can destroy a man. Let me tell you what I do know about you," Brannon continued. "You paid a Mojave Indian sixty dollars to let you cross the desert. Then you holed up on the Gila for two days at a cave above the Big Bend. After that you skirted Tucson and spent two nights at the Merry Mary in Florence. Then you rode the ridge along the White River reservation, had a gunfight with the Navajos near Mexican Wells where a couple of my deputies paid you a visit, and finally you crossed the Colorado near

15

Eagle Tower Mountain . . . how am I doin', Tap?"

Andrew coughed. "You knew all that?"

"Yep."

"Then why didn't you ride in with boys and arrest me? There was a bounty out, you know."

"I just didn't have the heart for it. I knew you didn't shoot that banker. I figured you were covering up for some lady, son."

"Don't 'son' me. You aren't that much older."

"That's the nicest thing anyone's said to me in years! Besides, I heard some old gal confessed to the crime a few years back, so they must have quit lookin' for you."

"Yeah . . . that keeps the law off my back. They even ruled that it was justifiable homicide. I suppose it didn't hurt any that she was pretty and blonde."

Brannon reached down for his foot.

"Keep your hands away from those boots!" Andrews shouted.

"Look, I need to straighten my broken toe . . . do you mind?"

"You broke your toe on that rock?" Andrews asked.

"Nope, it was already broken."

"How'd you do that?"

"I don't want to talk about it. Now can I get up?"

"You aren't goin' nowhere, Brannon."

"I thought we talked that out."

"We haven't solved nothin'! Stick them hands behind your back."

"What?"

16

"You heard me!" Andrews commanded.

Within a few minutes, Stuart Brannon sat on the front steps of the church with his hands tied to a post behind him. Tap Andrews shoved the fire to pieces and blanketed it dead.

Lord, I didn't figure Andrews for the revenge type. He's a little wild, maybe . . . but a good hand just the same. 'Course if I'd kept my mind, I'd have sighted this out before I came ridin' in like a kid goin' to a candy shop.

Andrews came over and sat down on the porch. "All right, Tap, you didn't shoot me on sight, so what's your plan?"

"Brannon, we tarry here until dark. Then we ride to a little cabin up in the mountains and wait for them to bring the money."

"What money?"

"Ransom money."

"Ransom?"

"Yep . . . figure ol' Stuart Brannon to be worth $5,000, don't you?"

"To whom?"

"The Honorable Governor of the Territory of Arizona, that's who."

"Now you don't expect me to believe a stretcher like that, Tap. You're not the kidnapping type."

"When a man loses all he has in a crooked card game, he's got to raise some finances mighty fast. And that means money, Brannon. I know you can get along without it, but the rest of us mortals need it to survive."

"Tap, I don't believe it. You're not that type."

"Don't moralize me, Brannon. Certain elements in this state are offering $10,000 to deliver you dead."

"Who?"

"Whiskey peddlers and would-be Indian agents, to name a few. And I hear some gunman from New Mexico named Trevor's out to collect on that."

"Trevor? He's in prison."

"Don't know nothin' about that. But he hasn't forgotten you either. 'Course those carpetbaggers never did me any favors. Besides, $5,000 will do me fine. Money isn't everything."

It was a long afternoon. Brannon and Andrews talked about everything from the cattle business, gunfights, good horses, and several mutual female acquaintances. Andrews refused to talk about letting Stuart go. Brannon refused to talk about his broken toe.

All the while they talked cow, Brannon was plotting an escape. He figured that once he mounted Dos Vientos, he could make a break somewhere along the trail.

Tap won't shoot me in the back. He's foolhardy maybe, but not mean. That pony of his will never catch me in a chase. I'll make it to the ranch and lose him there.

Lord, it's a mighty peculiar way for a man to spend his fortieth birthday!

The sun had dipped in the west, and the

distant mountains appeared as only a shadowy blur when Tap signaled that it was time to ride. Other than the rope that held his hands behind his back, Brannon figured it had been a pleasant enough conversation. Andrews grabbed his arm and helped him mount up on Dos Vientos. After swinging up on his own pony, he pulled the reins on Brannon's horse so that the two would ride side by side.

With Brannon's Colt tucked into his belt and his own still holstered, Andrews laid his Winchester across his lap.

"Well, Tap, it's your play. Where are we headed?"

"Right straight up that mountain."

"We going to ride all night?"

Andrews pushed his gray hat to the back of his head. "We're going to ride until I say we're stopping. Now don't get smart, Brannon. You make a break, and I'll have to collect the big money for deliverin' you dead."

Oh, the words are all correct. But you don't have the right tone. Tap, you're havin' a tough time with this. 'Course you are noted for gettin' a little reckless . . . especially when there's a lady involved.

Brannon figured that within a half hour they would actually be on Triple-B range, country that he knew like the back of his hand — even in the dark.

It don't figure . . . I know this country better than he does. There's no way he's goin' to trot me across my own place. 'Course he might have a gang waitin' for me there. Tap's pretty much a loner . . . but you never know. Gamblin' debts can toss you in with mighty poor company.

The stars were bright, the moon only a thin slice, and the wind still warm when they crested the range and started down on the back side of Brannon's Triple-B Ranch. The air smelled slightly of pines and cedars, but felt more like soured air that had been corralled in summer too long.

Brannon managed to loosen the ropes on his wrists a little, but it had cost him dearly with pain and rope burns. His biggest problem was trying to figure how to pull the reins away from Andrews and get them looped around the saddle horn.

Brannon broke the stillness of the night. "We're going to need to rest the horses."

"Yep . . . I suppose you're right." Andrews held Dos Vientos's reins tight as he dismounted and waited for Brannon to climb down in the dark.

"You'd better give me an arm so I don't fall on my face," Brannon suggested. Andrews pulled the reins over Dos Vientos's head and dropped them around the saddle horn. He reached out to help Brannon down, but at that moment Brannon spurred Dos Vientos wildly, and the two darted into the darkness.

It was all Brannon could do to stay mounted, clutching to the roll of the cantle with his bound hands. A gunshot crashed into the trees above his head, and he continued to spur the big black horse.

"Andrews," he mumbled. "That shot was too close!"

Charting a course through the trees and mountains by finding openings in the sky above him, Brannon raced down the slope for the trail back to his ranch. He leaned forward and stayed low as they crashed through trees and brush, his knees locked on the horses flanks.

Spotting a low branch at the last moment, Brannon threw himself at the horse's neck. That forced his still-tied hands up in the air. With a painful yank, he was lifted off the horse when the wrist ropes caught a branch. Crashing into the brush and boulders below, he rolled to his right, hoping to escape the hooves of Andrews's horse, which he figured would be only a few paces behind.

He found that the rope had broken off his wrists; his right shoulder throbbed; his face felt battered and bleeding, and his broken toe throbbed with a pain that made him want to scream.

But he didn't.

Neither did he hear or see any sign of Tap Andrews.

Come on, Tap. You're a better rider than that! There isn't any way you couldn't follow me this far . . . unless you didn't want to follow me!

Brannon struggled to his feet, brushed off his shirt, and groped for his hat in the darkness. He limped back out onto what he thought was the trail and paused to catch his breath.

If Andrews is sitting back there waiting for me to move, then I'd better not make a sound . . . but if . . .

"Tap, this is crazy," he heard himself mutter. Then he whistled. On the third whistle he heard Dos Vientos trot toward him. "That-a-boy! You certainly don't take after El Viento. He'd have been home by now!"

Adjusting the saddle, he yanked the cinch tight and retied the latigo. His left leg stiff, he found himself fumbling several moments for the stirrup.

"Brannon, you're gettin' old," he mumbled. Once mounted, he slipped his Winchester out of the scabbard and laid it across his lap. "Well, old boy, I don't know what in the world's going on, but we're headed home."

Setting his own pace, he cut across the ranch towards the back of the house. About a half mile from the buildings he pulled up.

"Smoke? Do you smell that fire, boy? It can't be from the church . . . and it can't be from this morning's cook fire. That would have gone out hours ago. Billy and Pete are in Prescott, and they surely won't be back until Monday."

Tap? He said others were on the lookout for me. Maybe he was trying to keep me away from an ambush. Maybe . . .

Brannon walked the horse slowly and quietly toward the darkened ranch house. He hobbled the black horse near the fruit trees and crept out toward the barn, the Winchester held tight in his right hand. He was halfway across the yard when he heard the sound of several horses in the corral. Muffled noises from the house caused him to spin back around.

They're in the house! It's a trap. There's no one on this earth going to ambush me in my own living room! I hope those boys are prepared to shoot because I'm going to bust in there blazin'.

Sneaking around to a side window, he glanced inside, but could see nothing but the stars reflecting off the glass.

It's a cinch they're all watching the front door! Well, boys, it's time for a surprise.

Brannon silently eased the window open and carefully lifted his painful right foot. Taking care not to crack the rifle against the window casing, he soon stood in the pitch dark of his own living room.

He thought he heard a whisper in the next room.

I'll step over to the table, drop down behind it, and wait until they reveal their locations. It ought to be about three steps in this . . .

It wasn't.

His right foot crashed into something immovable. He tripped over a short stool and slammed against hardwood floor. Brannon rolled quickly to his right, cocked the Winchester, and waited for someone to fire.

Suddenly a kerosene light flickered on near the front door. He shouldered his rifle to fire . . . a little child cried, and a deep voice boomed, "My word, Brannon, is this the way you treat guests!"

Brannon lowered the rifle and stared. "Fletcher?"

"Well," a woman's voice chimed in, it's obvious that Stuart hasn't changed much."

"Harriet?"

Then the youngster cried again.

"Now it's all right, honey. Uncle Stuart just needs to clean up a bit, that's all."

"Julie?" he choked. "Little Robert? Earl, are you here too?"

"Shoot, Mr. Brannon, we're all here," Earl replied as he hurried about lighting other lamps. "Everyone but Andrews, but I suppose he'll wander in shortly."

As the light flickered on, Brannon stood staring at the guests who crammed his living room.

"Doc and Velvet! Peter? Where's Rose?"

"She's in the back room with Sean's wife and our new little granddaughter." Peter Mulroney smiled.

"Sean's wife? Is that you, Sean?"

"Yes, sir, Mr. Brannon. I'm twenty now, you know."

"But what are you? . . . where did you all . . . why are you . . ."

A statuesque woman with gray streaks in her black hair, wearing a silver ruffled gown, stepped out into the light.

"We're here of course to celebrate a birthday." She smiled. "Now if El Patron wouldn't mind attending to himself slightly, we could get on with the festivities!"

"Victoria!"

She stepped to his side, threw her arms around him, and kissed him on both cheeks. "On second thought, it is fitting that you look like this. It is the way we all remember you!" She laughed.

"For my birthday? You came in just for my birthday?"

Velvet stepped up and clutched Brannon's hand. "It's not every day that Arizona's living legend turns forty. Most of us never thought you'd live this long. You should have heard the Stuart Brannon stories we have been amusing ourselves with while we waited."

"Yeah," Dr. Shepherd added, "some of them were even true!"

"You really must wash your hands and face," Harriet scolded. "Victoria has prepared a delightful supper, and the children can't wait to come and visit with you."

"Children?" Brannon still sounded stunned.

"Yes," Harriet replied. "Julie and Earl brought their three, and Rose and Peter have their granddaughter. Doctor Shepherd and Velvet had to leave theirs in Tres Casas. We left the baby with my sister in Prescott, but this is our little Stuart."

A four-year-old youngster walked over, wide-eyed, and studied Brannon's rifle that he still held in his hand.

"Uncle Stuart, is that gun loaded?"

Brannon reached down, hugged the boy, and laughed.

Within twenty minutes the entire party, including a recently arrived Tap Andrews, were seated at Brannon's huge oak dining table heaped with steaming food.

"Tap, I knew you weren't telling me everything! Kidnapping me? You didn't really think I — "

"All I needed to do, Brannon, was delay you so the rest could get to the ranch. 'Course you were movin' kind of puny on your own."

"I say, Brannon, that is a nasty limp," Fletcher observed. "Did you take a shot in the foot again?"

"He broke his toe," Andrews reported.

"Oh, my," Harriet Fletcher sighed, "how did you do that?"

"Don't ask," Brannon shot back.

"Well, if El Patron doesn't ask a blessing soon, all the food will be cold," Señora Pacifica insisted.

Brannon looked again at her warm smile and flashing eyes.

"*¿En Inglés o Español?*" he teased.

26

*Lord, I should have married her years ago . . .
I know I should have.*

"At your ranch in English." She smiled and bowed her head.

Brannon cleared his throat and then began. "Lord, I sure don't feel very old, but I do feel mighty obliged. These are my good friends . . . actually they're all family. And I'm sure grateful that You brought them here tonight. This just might be the best birthday I ever had. 'Course, Lord, I'm still a young man as You well know. Now, eh . . . bless this good food that Vickie and the others whipped up for us, and keep us safe in Your hands. Thanks, Lord. In Jesus' name. Amen and amen."

Brannon rubbed his calloused hand across his eyes as he finished. He glanced up at the others who were staring at him. "Must have got some dirt in my eyes when I tumbled off that horse," he muttered. "Tap, help yourself. Then pass that chicken *asada* this way . . . and watch out for those peppers. Victoria likes it spicy!"

Most had finished eating and were scattered in conversations throughout the room when Brannon heard a faint knock at the front door.

He started to stand. "Well, now, who else did you invite?"

"Sage Quilici sent her regrets, but she needed to stay in Phoenix with the judge. I think he's failing quite rapidly," Harriet reported.

27

"I'll get the door," Señora Pacifica offered.

Brannon sat back down, stretching his arms behind his head.

"Stuart," Señora Victoria Pacifica called, "there is an Indian boy here who wants to speak with El Brannon."

"Give him a little plate of supper," Brannon advised. "Things are gettin' tight this fall on the reservation, and I've been feedin' as many as I can."

"Oh, I don't think he's after something to eat," she announced with raised eyebrows. "He said he wanted to speak to his father . . . Stuart Brannon!"

TWO

Brannon jumped to his feet and limped to the door. Everyone in the room grew silent — all but the children who scurried behind Brannon and peered out at the young Indian standing in the darkness on the front porch.

The boy looked to Brannon to be about twelve years old, over four feet tall, and strong-shouldered. His thick black hair was cut straight across the back of his collar. His bangs hung just barely above his eyebrows. Brannon noticed his fairly worn boots, duckings, suspenders, and long-sleeved cotton shirt covered with plenty of road dust.

Brannon cleared his throat and gazed back at the boy's steady stare. "Eh . . . I'm Stuart Brannon, son . . . did you want to talk to me?"

"Are you The Brannon?" the boy asked.

"Yep." Sensing the boy's disappointment, he continued, "Were you expecting someone else?"

"Are you the Stuart Brannon who spent the winter in the deep snow of Broken Arrow Crossing Station?"

"Yep."

"Are you the Stuart Brannon who wrote all these letters?"

The boy reached into his shirt and pulled out

29

a neatly tied bundle of yellowing letters.

"Fletcher," Brannon called, "he's got all the letters I sent to Elizabeth!"

At that name, the boy broke into a wide smile.

"I am Littlefoot! Elizabeth is my mother! You are The Brannon, aren't you?"

"Littlefoot?" Brannon choked. "You're Littlefoot?"

Suddenly twelve years of memories, years of fruitlessly trying to contact Elizabeth in Idaho, Oklahoma, Florida, and Washington faded. In his mind was a little log cabin . . . Everett Davis . . . a courageous Indian girl . . . and a baby.

Without giving it another thought, Brannon grabbed the boy and hugged him tight. "Littlefoot! I never thought I would see you again!" he exclaimed.

"My mother told me you would be very pleased to see me!" the boy added.

"Come in, come in . . . everyone, this is Littlefoot. Fletcher, you remember Elizabeth and — "

"My word, Stuart, this is incredible . . . after all these years! Of course I remember the lad and his very heroic mother."

The children hung onto Brannon as he led them all back to the middle of the large ranch house living room.

"Are these your other children?" Littlefoot asked.

"These? Oh, no, they are my . . . my good friends. No, I don't have any children."

"You mean, you don't have any other children — besides me," Littlefoot corrected.

"Perhaps," Harriet interrupted, "perhaps you might like to explain this to us, Stuart?"

"Eh . . . well . . . there seems to be . . ."

"Oh, I can explain it." Littlefoot motioned with his hands. "You see, my mother and I left the cabin to visit her people the year I was born. But when we arrived, a war broke out, and we left with Chief Joseph. Then we were captured in the Bear Paw Mountains and sent to Oklahoma. After that some of us were sent to Florida."

Littlefoot shifted his weight back and forth from foot to foot as he talked. Brannon noticed that he was much lighter complected than his mother.

"Well, my father . . . The Brannon, tried to find us. I have many letters here that were sent to us. Do you know I can read and write?" He turned to Brannon.

"That's mighty fine." Brannon nodded.

"Mother didn't know how to reach Father. She sent several letters that others wrote for her. We had almost given up. But two months ago, we received all the letters at once. A man from Washington, D.C., brought them to us.

"In one letter was some money you had sent for our train tickets. So we left Florida and rode all the way to Durango, Colorado. From there we bought horses and rode toward Arizona. But the horses were poor, and they died in a sandstorm. Mother's sickness prevented her from going on, so I came ahead to find you. And here I am. Is this our home? I like this. Do all of these people live here also?"

"Eh . . . no, they are just guests," Brannon stammered.

"Your mother is not well?" Señora Pacifica asked.

"No, my mother is quite ill. In Florida she was very sick. She had malaria — and now the coughing sickness. She is so weak, I fear for her life."

"Coughing sickness," Dr. Shepherd interrupted. "You don't mean tuberculosis?"

"Yes, that is it! She coughs up much blood and is barely able to eat. I think we should hurry back to her."

"How long has she had this coughing sickness?" Dr. Shepherd asked.

"For more than two years, but she is getting much worse. She has to sit up most nights now."

"Where is she?"

"In the valley of the chimneys . . . among the Navajo," Littlefoot reported.

"That's near the Utah border," Brannon announced. "It will take several days to get there."

Littlefoot looked around Brannon at the food remaining on the table. "Yes, and she keeps saying that you will know what to do."

"Me?" Brannon probed.

"Oh, yes, she said, 'Littlefoot, your father, The Brannon, always knows what to do.'"

"Father?" Fletcher blurted out. "Look here, lad, I'm sure Stuart cares about you and your mother very much, but I can assure you he's — "

"Fletcher!" Brannon stopped him. "I'll handle this!"

"My word, Stuart, you aren't going along with this charade, are you?" Fletcher whispered.

"Vickie, would you take Littlefoot to the kitchen and see that he has plenty to eat?"

"Certainly," Señora Pacifica replied. She swooped over and engulfed the boy as Brannon had seen her look after countless others at her own hacienda.

"Edwin, I'd like a word with you on the porch." Brannon stepped outside into the dark of a starlit night, with the air hanging still, and found not only Fletcher, but the entire crowd following him.

"We aren't about to miss this," Julie Howland announced.

"Now," Fletcher spoke softly, "why didn't you tell the boy the truth?"

"Look, I don't have any idea why Elizabeth would tell the boy such a lie all these years, but I believe she had a good reason."

"Maybe," Harriet Fletcher added, "it was the only way to keep hope alive."

"Perhaps." Brannon nodded. "But I just haven't figured out how to tell that boy that his real father was an outlaw and murderer who

abused his mother. Rutherford would have sold them both for a gold coin. And," Brannon added, "I have no idea how to tell him that I was the one who killed his father."

"Well," Velvet Shepherd sighed, "what can we do to help?"

"Doc," Brannon said turning to her husband, "how far along is the tuberculosis?"

"Well, tolerance among the Indians is normally quite low. I'm surprised that she has lasted two years. For heaven's sake, why would the government send mountain Indians to Florida? Why anyone would ever go to Florida is beyond me!"

"So it could be pretty serious?" Brannon asked.

"Serious?" Dr. Shepherd replied. "If she's coughing up blood and not eating, she won't last until Christmas — especially in a cold Navajo hogan."

"Well," Brannon added, "I'm not telling the boy anything until I talk to Elizabeth."

"Won't that be falsely keeping his hopes alive?" Harriet Fletcher asked.

"He's had false hopes for twelve years now; a couple more weeks won't hurt. We'll ride up and bring her to the ranch. Maybe by then the Lord can show me what to do. He's the only one who can figure this thing out."

"Are you ridin' out tonight, Mr. Brannon?" Earl Howland asked.

He glanced around at those crowded next to

him. "No," he sighed, "ten years ago I would have ridden out in the dark. But we'll need some supplies, fresh horses, and a little rest first. Only a couple of you need to go with me."

"Oh, my," Fletcher stammered, "certainly if there was any way, but I've got to be at the consulate in San Francisco by Monday, and we promised Harriet's sister a few days in Prescott. Dreadfully sorry, Stuart."

"No . . . no," Brannon responded. "I didn't expect everyone to — "

"Oh, Stuart," Velvet sighed, "I do wish we had brought the children. They're staying with the neighbors, and we promised to return home quickly. We must catch the train in Tucson tomorrow evening."

Rose Mulroney spoke next. "I'm afraid we're in the same predicament as Velvet. I'm still teaching, you know, and I must report back to my class . . . perhaps Sean could stay?"

"No, he's got that freighting job on Wednesday," Peter Mulroney interjected. "A family man has to take all the work he can. I'm really sorry — "

"Don't think a thing about it," Brannon assured him. "I think Earl and I could probably . . ."

Earl Howland scratched the back of his neck. "Mr. Brannon, you know I've got to finish digging that well, or I won't have a cow on the ranch survive 'til the rains come. But I could sure ride over here and see that Billy and Pete take good care of your place."

"Yeah . . . that will help," Brannon mumbled.

"Count me in, Brannon, providin' you won't hold that skit I pulled against me," Tap Andrews announced.

"Thanks, Tap, you don't have anything to worry about . . . until you turn forty!" Brannon teased.

"I've got two hundred head of Mormon beef waiting for me in Cedar City," Andrews added, "so I have to ride that way anyhow. 'Course you'll have to haul on back here on your own."

"We'll pull out about sunrise. I figure to return in a week, ten days at the most."

"I will ride with you *también*," a soft female voice intoned.

Brannon turned to see Señora Pacifica now standing at the doorway.

"Where's Littlefoot?"

"Asleep."

"Asleep?"

"Yes, he was very tired, and now he sleeps on his father's bed," she declared.

"Vickie, I can't ask you to ride out there. It's kind of rough and — "

"And an *hombre* named Trevor is on the prowl, hoping to find the legendary Stuart Brannon," Andrews reported.

"Trevor?" Velvet Shepherd groaned.

"My word, is he still alive? I thought —," Lord Fletcher began.

"Trevor's of little concern," Brannon interrupted. "The truth is, it would be best not to travel with such a beautiful lady."

"Then I will stay here at the ranch and get things prepared for your arrival," Señora Pacifica suggested. "Ramon is not expecting me to return to the hacienda until the first of October."

"That'd be much appreciated." Brannon motioned the others into the house.

"Victoria Pacifica took Brannon's arm. "When Elizabeth arrives, you can always tell her I'm just the Mexican servant," she teased.

"You look no more like a servant," Brannon responded, "than Fletcher looks like a Frenchman."

"I say . . . ," Fletcher complained.

"I'm sorry to be cutting out on all of you like this," Brannon apologized. "It has been a mighty fine birthday. And plenty of excitement!"

"Stuart," Julie Howland mused, "have you ever had a quiet day in your life?"

The entire crowd howled.

"Actually," Fletcher continued, "I believe there was one afternoon back in '84 that Brannon had nothing at all to worry about."

"Yes, and I'll bet he was very bored." Velvet Shepherd giggled.

"Oh, my yes. Frightfully so," Lord Fletcher conceded.

"You know, Stuart, I'm glad you never change," Rose Mulroney added.

"Why's that?" Brannon asked.

"Look at us. Look around and what do you see?"

"My very good friends . . . and a scoundrel or two." He nodded and winked at Tap Andrews.

"No," Rose continued, "what you see is a roomful of people growing old. We're scattered around the country — raising children, settling into some sort of routine. But here's our Stuart, never changing . . . the round table is almost empty at Camelot. Only King Arthur is left."

"That's a little dramatic, isn't it?" Brannon insisted.

"No, I don't think so," Lady Harriet Fletcher concluded. "In our minds you will always be our hero — a gallant knight chasing off to defend righteousness. We need you to be that way. It gives us hope that the West might turn out to be a decent place to raise families after all."

"This is all sounding like a vat of corn syrup," Brannon huffed. "There's no use everybody getting sentimental. We'll just ride up there and bring Elizabeth back to the ranch. This dry climate might help her a little. That's all. It's the same thing any of you would do . . . you know, if you weren't busy with other important things."

"And I say," Lady Fletcher added, "it will be another exciting chapter in the life of El Brannon. It reminds me of a time many of us were here at the Triple-B."

"You aren't going to write a book about this one, too, are you?" Brannon quizzed.

"That, my dear Stuart, I promise to leave to the literary genius of Hawthorne Miller."

In the smiles and laughter of his good friends, Brannon suddenly found himself feeling extremely tired — and surprisingly — lonely.

He debated with himself whether to take a wagon out to find Elizabeth or whether to take a string of horses. Abandoning his house to his guests, he, Andrews, and Littlefoot camped in the bunkhouse.

Before a quiet, dry daylight entered the eastern sky, he was out in front of the barn saddling horses. Earl Howland and Tap Andrews soon joined him.

"You decide against the wagon?" Andrews asked.

"Yep. There still aren't many roads through that Navajo country," Brannon offered. "I figure if Elizabeth is too sick, we can travois her back to the Flagstaff corrals and rent a rig there."

"Leavin' at daylight?" Howland quizzed.

"Earl, you know me. I was never worth a dime sittin' around."

"I don't like the sounds of this Trevor thing," Howland cautioned.

"Well, I've spent almost every day of my life lookin' back over my shoulder." Brannon shrugged. "No reason to worry now. Besides, Trevor's mostly talk. His kind is part of the old

West, and things are changing fast. One of these days we'll get statehood, and I aim to be here to see it."

"Tap," Howland added, "you keep a close eye on Mr. Brannon. His mind is quicker than his body."

Brannon threw his arm around Earl Howland's neck and roughed up his hair. "One more old man joke, and I'll hogtie you and hang you in the smokehouse!"

The parade began about 6:00 A.M. A procession of sleepy-eyed children and women in dressing robes said their good-byes to Brannon, Andrews, and Littlefoot. Most of the men were dressed, as was Señora Pacifica, who personally bundled up an ample supply of food-stuff for the trip.

Brannon rode Dos Vientos. Behind him came a pack mule named Feathers, then a roan saddle horse for Elizabeth. Littlefoot rode next on a pinto called Six Bits, and Tap Andrews took a position in the rear of the string.

After a round or two of good-byes, Señora Pacifica halted the whole procession before it left the yard.

"Mr. Brannon," she said smiling, "I didn't arise at 4:00 A.M. and prepare all this food for a mere handshake and a tip of the hat."

"Eh . . . well, Vickie . . . you know the yard's kind of full of people and — "

"Come now," she insisted with flashing eyes,

"we're beyond the age to worry about what others think!"

Brannon climbed off the tall black horse and stepped to her side. Pulling off his hat, he slipped his arm around her waist.

"Stuart," she whispered, "please be careful. You cannot begin to imagine how important you are to me."

"Vickie . . . you know . . . sometimes . . ."

Her arm flung around his neck, and her kiss found his lips as those in the yard broke out in clapping.

"*Vaya con Dios,* cowboy." She blushed.

"*Y usted también.*" He nodded, remounted Dos Vientos, and led the string out of the yard without looking back.

Within a few minutes they settled into a steady caravan as they took the north road out of the ranch. Littlefoot spent much of the time riding off the trail, getting used to the pinto.

"Why do you call him Six Bits?" he asked Brannon.

"Well, when I was about your age, livin' down in Texas, I had a pinto a lot like him. The old man I bought the horse from called him Six Bits, so I kept the name. When I bought this one a few years back, I decided to call him Six Bits, too."

"Did he cost a lot of money?" Littlefoot quizzed.

"Why do you ask?"

The boy continued to ride alongside, but

41

glanced down at the saddle horn as he talked. "I thought that perhaps someday I could buy him for my very own."

"Buy him? Littlefoot, let's get something straight. You and your mother are going to be livin' right back there on that ranch with me. That is your horse right now."

"Really?"

"As of this day Six Bits, the horse, belongs to Littlefoot."

"Is that true?"

"Did you hear me, Tap?" Brannon shouted.

"Yep."

"Is my word good?"

"You can go to the bank on that," Andrews suggested. "That horse is yours, boy."

Littlefoot leaned forward and hugged the horse's neck and then sat up with a smile. This time, when he talked, he looked Brannon in the eyes.

"Back at the ranch, I was afraid," he admitted.

"Afraid?"

"I saw the way the Señora kissed you. I thought perhaps you did not want my mother for your wife anymore. You will not have two wives, will you?"

"Littlefoot, I can promise you one thing — I will never, ever have two wives! The Señora is just a good friend."

"She is a nice lady. I believe my mother will like her."

"I'm sure she will." Brannon nodded.

42

Within minutes, Littlefoot raced the horse far up the trail ahead of the others. Tap Andrews rode up beside Brannon.

"Normally, I ain't one to meddle, but it seems to me you're headin' for a sticky situation until you tell that boy the truth."

"You're right about that. But that Elizabeth is a smart lady who's been dealt a bum hand. I just want to hear her story before the whole thing falls apart. And I was serious about that horse. Even if the boy doesn't come back with me, it's his horse."

"Oh, I know that," Andrews acknowledged. "Listen, I've got another personal question that really isn't any of my business. But I'm goin' to ask it. How come you and the Señora have never gotten hitched?"

"Tap, that's a question I keep askin' myself every time I hold her in my arms. We came mighty close about eight, nine years ago. Probably should have. But Victoria's needed by a hacienda full of people down in the Sierra Madres. I just couldn't ask her to desert them and move up here. It wouldn't be fair."

"And you? Why don't you move south?"

"Well, I like to think that houseful of folks we left at the ranch, plus a few others, need me here in Arizona. Maybe I'm just kidding myself, but it sort of gives me a purpose in life."

"Still . . . you've got to think about yourself too," Andrews insisted.

"The way we figure it, sometimes the Lord

wants you to think about other people's needs instead of your own. I know it doesn't make sense to everyone. But it's not like we've never been married. Both of us are mighty fond of dwelling in the past."

"Well," Andrews concluded as he turned to ride to the back of the string, "I'm glad that wasn't my callin'."

Brannon shifted his weight in his saddle and took some pressure off his throbbing toe.

Lord, it sounded kind of noble when I talked to Tap, but it sure does make my heart feel anxious. Keep on remindin' me why I'm doin' this 'cause some days . . . some days sure are lonely.

It was on the third day out from the ranch that they broke out of the mountains and entered the desert. Other than the supper they chewed at the one cantina in Mexican Wells, most of their meals took place around a campfire. Without much instruction, Littlefoot tended the fire, Andrews the horses, and Brannon cooked.

Their first night on the red desert found them camped against the broken walls of an abandoned Navajo hogan. Brannon rose before daylight and scratched together a meager fire.

Most likely cold meals from here on. Nothin' left to burn up . . . 'course we might make Littlefoot's valley of the chimneys by tomorrow

44

night. Providin' we don't hit dust, Indians, or rattlesnakes.

Stuart Brannon had never met a sunrise he didn't like. And the ones on the desert were his favorites. Camp smoke, boilin' coffee, a whiff of sage, and the slightest hint of coolness in the air. The morning air always soothed his lungs.

Sitting with his back to the broken wall, he stared east and glanced at the last star hovering above the horizon where the sun would soon make an appearance.

Venus, I presume. Lord, it sure is quiet out here. No folks bustlin' about worried how they look and how much money they want. No cows bellowing for their calves. No dogs barking. No hungry coyotes howling for a meal. I always figured You came out here when You wanted a break. But that's just me talkin'. I know it's all beautiful in Your sight. But if it's all right with You . . . I'd appreciate if You kept a bit of this country barren. It's sure healthy for our souls.

The distant peaks turned from a black silhouette to a deep purple. The sky gave clues of turning blue when Brannon swished the last of the coffee in his tin cup and gulped it down, straining the grounds with his teeth. It was cold and bitter. He got to his feet to stir the fire. Setting the cup on the broken ledge behind him, he stooped over. A rifle shot splintered the silence. The punctured cup bounced across the fire.

45

Brannon hit the ground with his revolver drawn and crawled to the wall. Andrews sprang out of his bedroll, rifle in hand, and immediately tackled a bewildered Littlefoot who was half asleep, sitting up on his blanket.

Two more shots stirred the dust around the fire. Andrews and Littlefoot crawled over to Brannon who had pulled out his Winchester and was shoving cartridges into the breech.

"Who's out there?" Andrews called, trying to scan the horizon while staying below the top of the wall.

"Indians . . . outlaws . . . could be the Mormon militia . . . I don't know. Littlefoot, you keep down."

"I am not scared."

"You ought to be. Those are real bullets flying around us."

"I know how to shoot. My mother has taught me."

Brannon gazed at the boy for a moment, then motioned toward the pack supplies that lay up against the wall. "You take that scattergun, but don't pull the trigger unless I say so!"

Several more shots crashed about, keeping them pinned down and unable to return fire.

"Why didn't they sneak around to the open side and plug us?" Andrews questioned.

"No tellin'," Brannon answered. "Maybe they're a little short on courage."

"Then it don't sound like Indians to me," Andrews added.

Brannon moved to a better position. "I was thinking the same thing."

"Maybe just some bushwhackers," Andrews offered.

"Hey, at the wall!" a voice from across the prairie called. "We only want Brannon! The others can ride out!"

"Well, that lets out common outlaws and Indians," Andrews replied. "Where do you figure they are."

"Wasn't there a grove of dead cholla back there . . . nothing but spines and skeletons?"

"About a hundred yards back?"

"Yeah . . . we'll . . ."

"You others got three minutes to haul out of there!" a voice shouted. "Our score is with Brannon!"

"Trevor?" Andrews asked.

"Can't tell . . . yet. Littlefoot, when I tell you, you take that stick and raise Tap's hat up in the middle of this wall."

"My hat?"

"Yep. Tap, you holler at them. Then on the signal you fire at the cholla from that end of the wall, and I'll take this end. We won't be able to hit much, but we can keep them at a distance till we figure out something."

Andrews cupped his hands around his mouth.

"If I get up to leave, you'll shoot me down!" Andrews yelled at the attackers as he continued to move into position.

47

"We won't shoot ya, Mister," the voice hollered. "There ain't no money in it!"

Brannon nodded for Littlefoot to raise the hat. Immediately a thunder of shots blasted the hat and wall. At that moment Brannon and Andrews pelted the cholla grove with a rapid succession of .44 bullets.

A horse screamed in pain.

Someone cursed.

And the shooting stopped.

THREE

Andrews scrambled for his bullet-ridden hat as Brannon shoved more cartridges into his rifle. "They're mad now. Chances are they'll swing wide on all sides and make a charge," Brannon shouted. "Littlefoot, can you ride bareback?"

"Yes, of course."

"We'll fire another round at the cholla. You mount Six Bits and ride for the valley of the chimneys. Don't slow down until you are far away from here. We will catch up with you later."

"I am not afraid to stay," the boy protested.

"Do you mind your mother when she asks you to do something?" Brannon pressed.

"Yes of course, eh . . . most of the time." The last of the sentence trailed off to a whisper.

"Then you should mind me also." Brannon glanced back across the desert to the east. "Do you see that bluff? You can wait for us there . . . if anyone chases you, continue to the camp of the Navajos. We will catch up with you, I promise you that."

"I will go then," Littlefoot agreed.

"You ready, Tap?" Brannon called.

"Yep."

"Go, Littlefoot!" Brannon commanded. At that second he and Andrews again rolled to the edge of the wall and opened fire on the cholla grove. Brannon had fired four shots before he realized that the men had left their protection and were riding away from the scene to the west.

Tap Andrews stopped firing.

"Are they lightin' shuck?" he called.

Brannon stood up behind the wall and strained to follow the dust column that marked the retreating gunmen.

"Yeah . . . I reckon."

"You think it was Trevor?" Andrews asked.

"Nope. He would have put up more of a fight than that."

Andrews pulled off his battered hat and walked over to Brannon. "To tell you the truth, I've seen a house cat put up a better fight than that. I mean, a few potshots from across the desert. What kind of attack is that?"

"Well, Mr. Tapadera Andrews, either they are the world's dumbest ambushers, or they had no intention of shooting us."

"Then why did they do it?"

"Maybe as a warning, or maybe they just didn't have the heart for it." Brannon continued to scan the horizon.

"A warning? You mean, just to let you know you're a target?"

"Perhaps." Brannon let the hammer back down off his rifle and glanced around the camp. "Tap, you break camp, and I'm riding out to that dead horse and see what I can tell. We'll catch up with Littlefoot and then — "

"Won't need to do that," Andrews interrupted pointing to the Indian boy now riding back to camp. "You know, Brannon," Andrews needled, "that son of yours is a brave boy."

Brannon raised his hand as if to speak, but Littlefoot's return prevented him.

Within five minutes, they had all the horses saddled, gear packed, and were on their way across the desert. Andrews and Littlefoot led the way. Brannon dropped back to keep an eye out for any riders coming out of the west.

"It will be hard for them to sneak up on us in the daytime as long as we stay on this desert," Andrews shouted.

"Yep," Brannon called out. " 'Course they might be pushin' us instead of chasin' us. And now there's three of them on two horses."

Andrews reined around and rode back to Brannon. "You mean, a larger group might be on up ahead, and these were just trying to hustle us into an ambush?"

"The thought did occur to me," Brannon sighed. "Keep your eyes open, and hold us out on the flats."

Riding the desert was different from riding the mountains, and it didn't take long for the routine to become a rut. Ride two hours . . . dismount, loosen cinches . . . take a swig of water . . . walk an hour . . . take another drink, tighten cinchas . . . remount and repeat the process.

51

The sun had swung past the halfway point in the cloudless sky when they stopped in the shade of the western edge of a washout to eat. They didn't even attempt to find wood for a fire.

"Brannon, doesn't this seem a little strange?" Andrews questioned. "We haven't seen a soul since we left those bushwhackers. You'd think we'd come across a pilgrim or a prospector or at least some Navajo. This country isn't this wide open, is it?"

"Sort of makes you think that other folks know something you don't," Brannon allowed.

"We're not lost, are we?" Andrews asked.

"Well, we don't know exactly where we're goin', and we don't know exactly where we are, so how could we be lost?" Brannon joshed.

"This is not the trail that I traveled," Little-foot reported.

"Yeah . . . I suppose you stayed right at the base of those mountains." Brannon pointed to the south.

"How did you know?"

"Because that's exactly what I would have done . . . that's why we're out here. If someone is looking for us, they would look over there — not out here."

They rested only a short while and then walked the horses out of the arroyo and out across the desert.

It was late afternoon when Andrews reined up and waited for Brannon.

"Don't glance back, Stuart, but I do believe we have someone trailing us."

Continuing to ride east, Brannon nodded. "A single rider on a spotted horse slightly to the northwest?"

"You saw him?"

"About an hour ago."

"An hour? Why didn't you say something?"

"Well, there's nothin' much to say . . . he's not botherin' us."

"You think he's Navajo?"

"That would be my guess. Maybe we're getting close to their camp. Littlefoot, does any of this country look familiar?"

"It all looks the same," the boy spoke out. "And it all looks different."

Right before sunset, Brannon turned them back toward the mountain range to the south.

"We'll have to take our chances back in the hills. There's not enough out here for the horses to eat," he announced.

"How about that hombre behind us?" Andrews asked.

Brannon stopped Dos Vientos and glanced back. He could see no one. "We'll find out about him before long, I suppose." He motioned them forward.

Although Littlefoot scraped together some dry sage for fuel, Brannon declined to build a fire. Expecting trouble, he hobbled the horses and the mule and tied them to a picket line as well. There wasn't much in the way of grass even in

53

the hills, but he fed them half of the grain he had left and let them have a long drink of water.

They slept that night in the shelter of some boulders overlooking the horses. Brannon and Andrews took turns at night guard.

Sitting with his right boot off, Brannon tried to listen to the desert night. He heard Littlefoot's breathing, Andrews's restless tossing, an occasional shuffling of a horse's feet, and a dull ringing in his left ear that hadn't left him since the rifle shots of the morning.

"Stuart!" Andrews whispered. "I'll take a spell."

"I'm doin' all right."

"If we run into those bushwhackers, we'll both need some rest."

"Yeah . . . well, just for a little while," Brannon conceded.

"I sure could use a cup of coffee," Andrews complained.

"After daylight. Let's build a fire after daylight."

With his head propped on his saddle, Brannon closed his eyes, and his thoughts turned to Victoria Pacifica.

Lord, there's something real peaceful about knowin' that such a lady is taking care of the ranch when I'm gone. I guess it's been so long since Lisa's death that I forgot the feelin'. It's almost like a man can be in two places at once. If You could just help me figure how to transfer all her people up here to the Triple-B, maybe I could convince her to move.

A chilling thought hit his mind, and his body began to shake. He sat straight up so quickly that Tap Andrews cleared leather with his Colt and waved it in the darkness.

"What is it? Did you hear something?"

Brannon wiped the sweat off his forehead. "Sorry, Tap . . . it's nothin' here. A thought just hit me. If Trevor is serious about coming after me, he'll go to the ranch."

"And you're gone, so what?"

"Victoria's there! He could use her to get to me! She's gone through that before! I promised myself I would never get her in that kind of bind again. What am I doing? Why in the world did I encourage her to stay at the ranch?"

"She's got Pete and Billy there by now, and Howland said he'd be around."

"No, I've got to get her out of there, Tap. You've got no idea what that lady's been through."

"She seems mighty capable," Andrews replied, pushing the brim of his hat back with his revolver.

"Tap, I can't do it. Not again . . . not ever. You asked me why we never married. That's reason number one. It's the physical danger hanging around Stuart Brannon."

"I think you might be overplayin' this a bit."

"I must have been crazy!" Brannon moaned. "All those others with their peaceful family life

55

— it tricked me. My life is not that way. It's never been that way. It can never be that way!"

"And I think you need a little sleep."

Brannon jumped to his feet and began to pace. "Tap, there are experiences that a man can only go through once in life, and the second time will break him. Do you know what I'm shootin' at?"

Andrews holstered his gun and leaned his back against a large granite boulder. "Yeah . . . I know."

"Listen, Tap, at daylight I want you to ride north. When you hit the railroad tracks, go east and you'll come to a fuel station called Medicine Hat. They'll have a telegraph there. You've got to send a wire to Prescott and have them ride down to the ranch. Tell Victoria that I need her to return immediately to the hacienda. Tell her that her life could be in danger."

"Brannon, I still say you're overreacting."

"Tap, will you do it for me?"

"Of course. Now are you goin' to get some rest, or do we just palaver all night?"

Brannon lay back down and closed his eyes. The ground felt hard. His toe hurt. His left shoulder kept cramping. There was a tingling in his ear. Road dust covered him like a grimy blanket. Visions of Trevor holding a gun on Señora Pacifica haunted his dreams.

He slept very little.

A clean-burning fire, hot coffee, and sizzling

56

salt pork helped them greet the morning. Littlefoot had saddled Six Bits and was riding in
circles around the camp before breakfast.
Brannon motioned him to come in and eat.

"Any sign?" he asked the boy.

"No. No one came close to camp," Littlefoot
reported.

For several minutes there was no sound
other than the scraping of tin plates and the
smacking of lips. Finally, Andrews saddled his
horse and mounted up. "You sure you don't
want me to circle back after I send that telegram?"

"Nope. You go on and get those cows before
the Mormons change their minds. Where did
you say your ranch was?"

"Three days west of Big Trouble, Montana,"
Andrews explained.

"Well, save a bunk 'cause one of these days
I'll come a visitin'," Brannon insisted.

"I'll tell you what — if Arizona gets statehood
before Montana, we'll toss a party at your
ranch. But if Montana gets there first, you
come to a party at my ranch."

"It's a deal, Tap . . . thanks for ridin' out in
the desert with me."

"I didn't do nothin'."

"Well, you scared the daylights out of me back
at the church." Brannon faked a scowl.

"Come on, Stuart, the only thing that's scared
you lately is the thought of harm coming to the
Señora."

"Andrews, get out of here," Brannon prodded. "There's nothin' I hate worse than a guy who can see right through me."

Brannon's calloused hands hardly felt the cold steel of the bit or the warm moisture on Dos Vientos's tongue as he slipped the headstall onto the black gelding. Hooking a stirrup over the horn, he hefted the saddle, and a sharp pain shot down his left shoulder and arm. His legs were stiff, and he hobbled as he circled the horse.

"Does your toe still hurt?" Littlefoot asked.

"That plus too many years of sleepin' on the ground," Brannon groaned.

"Are we going out in the desert today?" Littlefoot asked.

"No, we'll take our chances in these hills. I believe we should come to the south side of the valley of the chimneys today."

"Yes, Mother will be very happy."

Brannon and Littlefoot broke camp and rode up the trail with the pack mule and spare horse in tow. For the rest of the morning, they rode side by side. Deep in conversation, Littlefoot seldom took his eyes off Brannon. With his own eyes constantly scanning the horizon, Brannon quizzed the boy.

"Littlefoot, where did you learn to read and write?"

"When we were taken to Florida, two women, the McGuire sisters, came to live with us and teach school."

"What did you learn?"

"I learned the names of all the Presidents from Washington to Cleveland."

"What else?"

"I learned my multiplication tables. And how to read McGuffey's. And all about Jesus."

"They taught you the Bible?"

"They taught me to read the Bible. My mother taught me what it meant."

"How about hunting and fishing and things like that? Did you learn those in Florida also?"

"Yes, my mother's people taught me many things, but the Seminoles taught me how to catch alligators."

"Your mother's people?" Brannon asked. "You mean, your people, the Nez Percé?"

"They are not really my people," he answered with his head down.

"What do you mean?"

"I am a breed. You know that. I do not belong to any people . . . except for you and Mother," the boy confessed.

Lord, this isn't going to be easy. Why did she do it? Why did she tell him a lie?

"Did I tell you I know how to grow corn?" Littlefoot blurted out.

"No, you didn't."

"They taught the girls to sew and the boys how to raise corn."

"Well, that's good," Brannon encouraged him. "Now what did you learn about Jesus?"

"He is my mother's God, you know," Littlefoot replied.

"Yes, I know that."

"Is He your God too?"

"Yep. I think that's probably a pretty good way to put it."

"Then . . . I think He shall be my God also."

Brannon smiled. "I'm sure it will make your mother happy."

"My mother," Littlefoot added, "has not been happy in a long, long time. She has had a very hard life, you know."

"You're right there, son." Brannon nodded.

"Tell me," Littlefoot continued, "why would my mother's God allow her so many heartaches?"

"Well, I . . . I suppose," Brannon stammered, "it's better to think about where we're headed rather than on the trail we have to take to get there."

"You mean Heaven?"

Turning in the saddle, Brannon searched for anyone following them. "Yeah. I think that's what I mean."

"My mother speaks often of Heaven lately. Sometimes I think she would rather go there than stay with me."

Brannon hunted for words to say, but nothing came to mind. After several minutes of listening to the slow, lonely sounds of their horses' hoofbeats, he was almost relieved to spot someone following them.

"Littlefoot, we will circle into those boulders. I want you to lead that horse and old Feathers on up the mountain, but keep out of sight. When you get to the edge of the desert, break into a gallop. In the dust, he won't be able to tell how many riders there are."

"You will drop back behind him?"

"Yeah, that's the plan."

"Are you going to kill him?"

Brannon stared at the boy.

"No, I don't plan to kill anyone . . . ever."

Littlefoot rode out of sight, and Brannon, still mounted on Dos Vientos, drew his Colt and spun the chambers, making sure the hammer was set on the empty one.

Lord, if our baby had lived, he would be . . . just a year older. I could be teachin' him to hunt, and brand, and rope. And Lisa would be . . . what am I doin'? I just sent a kid up there to do a man's job! Protect him, Lord.

The sound of hoofbeats on the rocky mountainside broke into his thoughts. He could hear a ring of metal striking stone and the jingle of pans.

He's not an Indian! Sounds like a peddler.

The noise stopped before the rider rode into view. Brannon slipped down off Dos Vientos and crouched behind more rock further up the hill.

"Ah hah!" a man yelled and jumped from behind a rock in front of the big black horse waving a rifle at the riderless mount. Dos

Vientos reared up and then darted toward the desert floor.

The gray-haired man stumbled backwards and fell to the ground. His gun discharged, the bullet ripping through the flesh on the back side of his right thigh.

"Mercy, mercy! I shot myself! . . . I shot myself! I'm goin' to die right here among the snakes and scorpions!" he cried.

With his revolver cocked and pointed at the man's head, Brannon stepped out from behind the rocks. "You make a move for that gun, and you'll die a whole lot sooner than you figured. Now hold still, and I'll give you a hand."

"What? Help from a claim jumper!" the old man shouted. "I'd rather take help from a — "

"What are you talkin' about, old man?" Brannon moved in closer but kept the revolver pointed.

"I been followin' you for two days. I seen that Indian boy leadin' you to my claim. You don't fool me. You won't get my diggin's. I'll kill ya first!" he shouted.

"Diggin's? Do you mean to tell me you found color out here?" Brannon quizzed.

"I ain't sayin'," the old man hollered, crawling over toward his rifle.

Brannon moved quickly to pick up the weapon.

"Give me my gun!" the man yelled.

Littlefoot broke into view leading the other animals. "I came back when I heard the shot," he called. "Did you need to shoot him?"

"Nope, I didn't need to. He did it for me."

"He shot himself?"

"Yep."

"It was an accident. If that black horse of yours hadn't spooked — it's all your fault," he yelled at Brannon. "I'm laying here bleeding to death, and you won't give me my gun!"

"Littlefoot, go round up Dos Vientos," Brannon called. "Old man, you got two choices. You can hush up and let me bandage that leg for you. Or I'll toss your rifle into those boulders and ride on out of here leavin' you to the buzzards. Now you make up your mind what it's goin' to be!"

"It don't matter to me. I'm a dyin' anyway!" he moaned.

"The bullet only grazed your leg. I've seen worse wounds on a widow after a barn dance. Now do you want my help or not?"

"Well, it couldn't hurt to have you wrap my leg . . . 'course that don't give you no part of my claim! It's all mine! Ever' bit of it's mine."

"You got any alcohol to pour into this wound? We ought to burn it out before I wrap it."

"I ain't wastin' good alcohol on a scratch," he insisted.

"Suit yourself." Brannon wrapped the wound with the man's bandanna. "Now you listen up. Me and the boy are riding over these mountains to meet some . . . eh . . . some friends. We couldn't care less where your claim is or what it's worth. If you insist on followin' us, I'll hogtie you to a cactus. Now have you got that clear?"

"You expect me to believe a bushwhacker?"

"Bushwhacker? You're the one following me. You're the one who jumped over the rocks waving a gun yelling and screaming."

"And you were layin' low plannin' on gunnin' me down and taking my claim."

"Is your claim in the valley of the chimneys?"

"Of course not," the old man groused. "That valley's full of Injuns."

"Well, that's where I'm going. Now if you promise not to follow me, I'll promise not to follow you."

"You really ain't headin' for the peaches?"

Brannon looked back at the old man.

"Did you say peaches?"

"I didn't say nothin'!"

Littlefoot returned with all the horses, including the old man's, which was laden with prospecting gear.

With the old man still lying in the dirt, Brannon led the prospector's horse about thirty feet down the trail and tied it off to a jagged rock.

"Your rifle's in your scabbard," Brannon reported. "You're on your own."

"I cain't mount up with this wounded leg."

"You're going to be surprised what you can do," Brannon insisted. "And don't worry, we're not headed toward any orchard!"

"I didn't say nothin' about peaches," the old man shouted as they rode off.

Brannon kept a close eye out to see if the man was following them, and when assured that he wasn't, he led Littlefoot straight up toward the crest of the mountain range they had been skirting.

"The valley of the chimneys is over this mountain, isn't it?" Littlefoot asked.

"Yep."

"Why did the old man talk about peaches?"

Brannon looked at the boy and realized that he had gone all day without remembering that the boy was Indian. "Oh, that old man has probably been wandering out here in the sun so long he's forgot who he is and what he's doing. The sun and the gold will do that to you."

"But why talk of peaches? They can't grow fruit out here in the desert."

"Well, I'll tell you . . . I don't know of any peaches anymore. But about twenty years ago, while the war was raging back east, the Navajo had a nice little peach orchard up here in Canyon De Chelly. But the soldiers had orders to move them all to New Mexico so they came in and chopped down the peaches. Like to broke their hearts, so I hear. I've sure never heard of any other peaches, but I don't suppose the Navajo would want to tell anyone about them, would they?"

The sun was low in the west when they crested the mountains, and the tall spires of

65

the 900-foot-high red sandstone columns cast long shadows across the valley floor. Stale air hung like a blanket that needs to be beaten. Brannon remembered with fondness the chill of fall air high up in La Plata Canyon in Colorado.

"All right, Littlefoot, where is that Navajo camp where your mother is staying?"

"Down at the base of the one they call the Spider."

Brannon shoved back his hat and smeared the dust on his forehead. "The Spider?"

"Yes, the Navajo say that when children misbehave, their parents tell the woman on Speaking Rock across the canyon, and she informs the spider on the other column, who then crawls down and grabs the naughty children. The spider takes them up to the top and eats them. That's why it's white on top. It is the bones of children who disobeyed their parents."

"That's quite a stretcher." Brannon grinned.

"Yes, but it keeps the young children obeying their parents," Littlefoot replied. "Let's hurry. I know Mother will want to see us both!"

"Littlefoot, let me teach you a lesson about the West. Until this land tames down, you can't afford to be in a hurry — no matter what the situation."

"Do you mean, we are not going to race into camp?"

"Look down the slope of this mountain and what do you see?"

"It is bare — nothing but rocks no bigger than your fist."

"Yep. Just the right size to cause a running horse to trip."

"So we must go slowly?" the boy asked.

"Yes, and do you see any smoke at the base of that column where the camp is supposed to be?"

"No."

"Well, neither do I. It's suppertime, and no one's fixing a meal. Either they are gone . . . or . . ."

Littlefoot stood in the stirrups and gazed toward the tall shadowy column. "Or what?"

"Or they are expecting trouble. So what would you do if you were sitting there expecting trouble and saw several horses come galloping up in a cloud of dust?"

"Shoot at them, I suppose," the boy answered.

"That's why we are going to take it slow," Brannon announced.

"I must get to my mother. She will be quite worried."

"Here's what you can do. Ride halfway up that mountain slope and go along even with the valley. Stay behind the rocks if you can, and take a look into that camp. Perhaps you can see why they're hiding."

Littlefoot kicked Six Bits and trotted up into the boulders. Brannon continued to lead the horse and pack mule on out to the main trail up the valley. He pulled out his Winchester, cocked it, and laid it across his lap.

Lord, I would like to find Elizabeth and get this matter settled. And I'd like to think the time is coming when I only have to fire this old Winchester at four-legged beasts. Someday a man ought to be able to mount up and ride without packing any gun at all.

Several miles from the towering rock he pulled up behind some boulders and waited for Littlefoot. He scanned the horizon.

There were no leaves flapping in the wind. There were no leaves. No trees. No breeze. Absolutely no movement at all.

It's like walking into a motionless painting.

After a ten-minute wait he heard a horse up on the mountain, and within seconds Littlefoot came into view.

"Mother is not there! She is gone! I don't know what they have done with her!"

"Whoa!" Brannon cautioned. "Start from the beginning. Is the camp empty?"

"No, there are six armed men there, but they are not camped. They are hiding in the rocks."

"Hiding? Do you mean they are looking this way and have rifles pointed?"

"Yes, did you see them?" Littlefoot asked.

"Only in my mind. I believe they are waiting for me. This is where the others are pushing us."

"The others?"

"The ones who shot at us back at the broken hogan. They wanted to pin us down in between."

68

"How did they know you would come here?"

"I've been wonderin' about that myself. The only one out here who knows where we're headed is you, me, and Andrews."

Littlefoot scratched his neck. "And the old man . . . Mr. Peaches! You told him not to follow us to the valley of the chimneys."

"That was a dumb mistake! You're right. If they ran across that wounded old man, he'd be happy to send them our way!"

Littlefoot stood in his stirrups and searched the desert below. "Where is my mother?"

"You didn't see any sign of the Navajo?"

"No, but I was very far away!"

"Then these men have chased them off or . . ."

"Or killed them!" Littlefoot sobbed.

Brannon stared at the tear-streaked boy.

She is all he has in this world . . . and he is all she has.

"Listen. The Navajo are brave and wise people. Your mother is very courageous. They probably left camp ahead of these hombres and are quartered some other place. We will find them, I promise you. We will look until we find them."

"When? When will we go look?" Brannon noticed desperation in Littlefoot's voice.

"The first thing we need to do is try to get out of here before those boys with the rifles spot us."

"Do you mean we are to turn around?"

"Nope. The others are probably still back

there. What we're going to do is ride straight up that rim." Brannon pointed up the mountain with his rifle.

"But they will see us up there!"

"Yep."

"And they will follow us."

"I hope so."

"Why?"

"Because I reckon somewhere down around that pillar is a sign as to what direction your mother and the others went. But we can't find any clues until those men leave."

"So we will have them follow us?"

"Yep, that ought to draw them away."

"But how will we get back to the valley of the chimneys if we stay on this mountain?"

Brannon looked up at the steep, barren red sandstone cliff ahead of them. A single white cloud seemed to be caught at the top of the pillar called The Spider. The mountain offered no trees and little hope of concealment until they reached the top. Grabbing tight to the lead ropes of the mule and spare horse, he kicked Dos Vientos in the flank and began the ascent.

"I sure am hoping to have that figured out by the time we reach the rim."

FOUR

They know more about me than I know about them. They were waiting for me to ride up. They found me at the hogan . . . and I'm not even sure it's Trevor.

"Here they come!" Littlefoot shouted. "What will we do?"

Brannon glanced to the north. A spiral of desert dust rose next to the base of the giant stone chimney.

"We just keep climbing this mountain. We should be able to keep ahead of them."

"But they will be running their horses. Shouldn't we be in more of a hurry?" Littlefoot urged.

Brannon noticed the boy's dark eyes dart nervously across the landscape.

"They will soon tire of running up this slope. Either they will get off and walk the horses or ride them into the ground. As long as we keep moving, we can keep ahead of them."

"Are they the same as the ones at the hogan?" Littlefoot kicked his boots into the pinto's ribs and hurried to keep up.

"Some of them must be."

"How did they get ahead of us?"

"I suppose they circled around the mountains. They probably figured we'd be lookin' back — not forward. They were right." He pointed on up ahead. Do you see where that big boulder hangs out over the slope?"

Littlefoot shaded his eyes as he stared into the treeless reddish-brown mountain.

"Yes, I see it."

"Well, that's where we're aiming. You lead the horse, and I'll take the pack mule."

"Will we stop there?"

"Only to rest the horses and size up the situation," Brannon replied.

He could tell that the riders were gaining on them, but he held his pace back to save the animal's strength. The sun was lowering toward the ridge of the mountain, and soon it would be right in their eyes.

The desert air was dry, and Dos Vientos quickly began to lather up as they climbed the slope. Brannon could smell the wet wool aroma of the woven Navajo saddle blanket. Soon he was standing on loose red rock, hiking, tugging on the reins to get the animals to follow. Sweat rolled off his forehead, splashing on his shirt, and he could feel the throbbing of his foot as if the toe itself were the size of his boot. His throat, caked with a fine red dust, felt dry and raw.

He wiped his forehead on his shirt sleeve and jammed his black hat back on his head. When he reached the gigantic boulder overhang, he noticed that Littlefoot had tied off the horses and had climbed up to scout the horizon.

"What do you see?" Brannon called, as he dug an empty sack out of his pack and began to rub down Dos Vientos.

"I think some are turning south. The others are waiting for something."

"They're waiting for their horses to recover."

"Will we wait for them here?" Littlefoot inquired.

"Nope. We will gain some ground now. They will not be able to see us for a while. That boulder and the sunlight will block their view."

Littlefoot slid down off the rock and grabbed up the reins of his pinto and the lead rope of the other horse. "When do we go to the pillar and look for sign of my mother?"

"When we lose these hombres."

"And when will that be?"

"After dark. We'll hold them back until dark and then ride straight out that rim to the little mesa by the old Spider column."

"Won't they follow us?"

"Nope."

"Why?"

"Because our tracks will be hidden, and they know no one has ever descended from that part of the mountain."

"I don't understand."

"They will assume we are going back out into the desert on the west side of the mountain. Unless I miss my guess, those going to the south are circling around the mountain right now. They think we will have to come down on the east or the west, but we will come down right at the north by the column."

"But I thought you said it was impossible to descend there."

"I didn't say it was impossible . . . I just said it's never been done," Brannon replied.

An hour later Littlefoot and Brannon stood among the boulders on the crown of the mountain. The vista to the west was straight into a setting sun, and the blinding light blocked whatever view there might have been.

The view to the east was almost beyond Brannon's imagination. From that point he could see twelve tall columns of red stone spires in Littlefoot's so-called valley of the chimneys. Each now cast a long black shadow on the eastern mountains. Mirages of shimmering water lay scattered on the desert horizon. They danced like dreams over the dry landscape that seemed magnified in size and proximity.

A thin strata of clouds high in the sky now reflected a pinkish orange. The shady side of the mountain on which they stood took on a deep purple. If it weren't for the procession of gunmen scratching their way toward them, Brannon would have crawled up on the rocks and watched in silence until nightfall.

"Littlefoot, people back in the states would not believe it if you tried to describe this scene. They can't imagine either the colors or the enormity of this view. Take a good look . . . there's only two or three times in a man's life that he gets to see something like this."

After a moment, Littlefoot pointed to the men coming after them. "I do not think they are enjoying the view."

"That's the trouble." Brannon smiled. "Some men take their work much too seriously."

"I only see six men."

"The others are circling the mountain. If they ride all night, they should be at the west side about daylight."

"Then they will think they have us trapped up here."

"That's what we want them to think. Dig through our supplies and find anything extra that will burn. We want to have a fire."

Littlefoot looked puzzled. "For what purpose?"

"To let them know where we are." Brannon pulled out both his rifle and his shotgun.

"We will fight them?"

"No . . . we will just draw the lines here."

"Draw the lines?"

"We'll let them know if they come any closer, they'll get shot. That'll keep them until daylight."

"And what will we do at daylight?"

"Ride after your mother." Brannon cocked the Winchester and took a position behind a large boulder. "Now you stay down in those rocks and build yourself a fire."

The vibrant colors of the desert sunset had melted into the gray twilight by the time the riders below came out of the rocks and stood staring at a loose rock clearing that separated them from Brannon and Littlefoot. One of the men, in a tall Texas hat, dismounted and started to lead his horse across the opening.

Two quick rifle shots from Brannon's Winchester sent all six men diving back behind the rocks. Seeing that Littlefoot had a small fire smoking away, Brannon called the boy to his side.

"Littlefoot, you take the shotgun over to those rocks." He pointed to the south side of the fire. "You stay hidden, but when I signal you, you squeeze the trigger on that shotgun."

"What do you want me to aim at?"

"It doesn't matter. You couldn't reach halfway across the clearing with the gun anyway."

"So why do I waste a shot?"

"I want them to think about what they're facing. They need to know that there's more than one person up here shooting and that if they try sneaking up in the night, they just might face a scattergun."

"So when do I shoot?"

"I will fire two shots from my Colt. Then you count out loud to three and let her blast. While you're counting, I'll climb that boulder, and then I'll fling a couple shots from the rifle."

"Will they think there are three of us?"

"Maybe . . . but at least it will give them

something to discuss for a while."

Littlefoot moved to the far side of the smoking fire. Bracing his feet among the boulders, he placed the shotgun against his right shoulder and aimed it in the general direction of the pursuing gunmen.

"Are you ready?" Brannon called.

"Yes."

Brannon pulled off two quick rounds with the Colt revolver, knowing full well the lead would fall far short of the men.

Littlefoot began to count, "One . . . two . . ."

Brannon scurried up the rock to the highest boulder. "Three!" The blast from the shotgun echoed down the mountain and sent Littlefoot staggering back.

The distant popping sound of several wide shots fired in return came as Brannon fired the Winchester twice, making sure the bullets came close to the gunmen. Then he slid down off the rocks, dropped his rifle, grabbed his right leg, and rolled over by the fire groaning.

"Are you shot?" Littlefoot cried.

Brannon tugged his boot off and smeared back tears of pain from his eyes.

"I wish I was shot. It's my toe. I cracked it on the stock of my rifle when I stumbled."

"I think you should cut a hole in your boot so that it does not pinch your toe," Littlefoot suggested.

"And I think I ought to just shoot the thing

off." Brannon frowned. He noticed Littlefoot's eyes grow wide.

"I didn't mean it," Brannon quickly clarified. "I was just teasing . . . you know, a joke?"

"My mother was right," Littlefoot announced.

"About what?"

"She told me that The Brannon is a very brave and very wise but also a very stubborn man."

"Why did she say that?"

"I believe it was when my behavior reminded her of you." Littlefoot shrugged. "You know, I miss her very much. When will we go down this mountain?"

"In the next couple hours. The moon's been coming up about midnight. We will have to be out of sight by then."

Littlefoot looked up at Brannon. "How do you know when the moon rises?"

"Because . . . The Brannon is very wise!"

By the time it became totally dark, Brannon and Littlefoot had eaten the last of Señora Pacifica's tortillas and rested behind the protection of the rocks. They sat well away from the tiny fire.

"Load up our gear on that roan. I'm going to leave old Feathers here," Brannon commanded.

"Why are we leaving the mule?"

"It might slow them down. At daylight, when they venture out across that clearing, they will

78

see the mule and think we're still in camp. Besides, I don't think I could get the mule to plunge off that point of the mountain any-way."

"Will the horses?"

"I hope so." Brannon didn't look at the boy but rather led Dos Vientos and the roan horse out into the night. "Can you see the way I am going?" he whispered back at Littlefoot.

"Yes . . . I have very good eyes. I can spot an alligator at night in the swamps of Florida."

"Well, let me know if you see an alligator!" Brannon teased.

If he'd had plenty of time and supplies, Brannon would have wrapped a straw-stuffed sack around each of the horses' hooves.

But he didn't have any straw.

Or sacks.

Or time.

A slight breeze blowing right up the mountain from the east gave him hope that the sound of their departing horses could not be heard.

They reached the point of the mountain in about an hour. At that place it sloped down about fifty feet. Then it raised back up to form a very small mesa about the size of a plaza. Even in the darkness, they could see the outline of the descent in front of them.

"Will we ride down?" Littlefoot questioned.

"We will try to ride down. If you start to fall, scramble off on the right side. Don't go straight over the horse's head, or he might roll on you."

"Is the Brannon scared?"

"The Brannon is very wise and courageous," Brannon mimicked.

"And stubborn. Are you scared?"

"Yep."

"So am I."

"You must go first," Brannon cautioned, "so that I'm sure you aren't stranded up here." Both of them mounted their horses, which were prancing nervously.

"Could we go at the same time?" Littlefoot gulped.

"Hold on, partner!" Brannon called and slapped his hat at the rump of Littlefoot's pinto. Spurring Dos Vientos and tugging the lead rope of the roan, Brannon, too, plunged over the edge of the dark precipice.

Lord, I sure hope this isn't as dumb a stunt as it looks!

For the next several moments Brannon had no idea in the world what was happening to Littlefoot. Dos Vientos braced his front feet, tucked his back ones under himself, and stayed upright in the slide. About fifty feet down the grade, Brannon strained through the darkness and saw the roan lose its footing and start to tumble.

He had unconsciously held onto the lead rope on the other horse and was suddenly jerked from the saddle. Quickly releasing the rope, he grabbed the saddle horn and jammed his boots deep in the stirrups to try to keep from falling off.

Finally, losing his grip, he tumbled off on the left side of Dos Vientos, but his right foot was stuck in the stirrup, which now pulled up over the saddle and pinned his leg against the horse's side. Brannon was dragged upside-down and backwards down the mountain.

He kicked at the boot furiously and grew dizzy with the pain of his broken toe. Finally his boot gave way, and his foot slipped out. He and the horse continued to slide to the base of the steepest part of the mountain. Shaking the dirt out of his clothing and limping on his bootless foot, he checked out Dos Vientos. Finding him intact, he painfully re-sat the saddle, mounted the animal, and began to search for Littlefoot.

"Brannon!" he heard a faint voice call.

"Littlefoot, where are you?"

"Over by my mother's horse."

"Are you all right?" Brannon called.

"Yes, I stayed on the pinto. We are fine, but this roan is in bad shape."

Brannon unlaced his saddlebags and dug out some matches. Lighting one, he hovered near Littlefoot and the downed horse.

"She broke her leg!" Brannon announced.

"You do not look so well yourself." Littlefoot pointed to Brannon's ripped shirt and bootless right foot.

"I'll survive, but this horse won't. I'll have to . . ."

Lord, if I shoot this horse, it will give away our position. It's not right. I can't let the horse suffer. I've got to.

From the distance, Brannon heard several shots fired at their former location. Immediately he pulled his Colt and shot the suffering horse.

The speed of the event caused Littlefoot to jump back. "Won't they hear us?" he blurted out.

"Maybe . . . but maybe it just blended in with the echoes of the canyon. We've lost most our supplies, our horse, and our mule, and . . ."

"And you lost a boot."

"Yeah, but we're out of that ambush. Now let's ride to the base of the column."

They were still several miles from the former campsite of the Navajos, but the descent was much more gradual. They reached the tall pillar within an hour and rested at its base in the moonlight. Brannon stayed awake most of the rest of the night, waiting for riders in the shadows.

There were none.

At the first light of day, he scouted the former Navajo camp on foot, limping about looking for signs. He had Littlefoot ride out into the valley and look for traces of his mother and her party. Brannon found absolutely nothing. Finally he rode out toward Littlefoot trying to keep the red pillar between himself and the men back up on the mountain.

"Did you find any tracks?" he asked Littlefoot.

"I can't make out any fresh tracks on this side of that dry wash," the boy reported.

"What about on the other side."

"The trail is over here, not on that side."

"That's why, if they were leaving in a hurry, they should travel over there. Fewer people would go clear over there to follow them."

Riding across the sandy wash lined with weak-looking sage no taller than a rabbit, Brannon spurred his horse up the far bank and out onto the red- and yellow-streaked desert.

"Littlefoot! Over here!" he called.

The boy galloped to his side. "What is it?"

"A dozen ponies are riding south back into the heart of Navajo land . . . but look . . . one horse is going north."

"What is up there?"

"Sooner or later it must lead to Utah."

"Mother wouldn't go that direction. It is further from your ranch. Besides she was very ill. I do not think she could ride at all. I especially do not think she would try it alone."

"Well," Brannon said still staring at the tracks, "your mother is very courageous and very wise . . . and very stubborn."

"Why would she go back?"

"To find you . . . or to find friends . . . maybe

it was the only choice she had."

"Look!" Littlefoot shouted. "Do you see those three rocks piled up? It is a message from my mother."

"It's a marker, all right, but who knows who put them there? It could have been anyone," Brannon cautioned.

"My mother — she always leaves me a message like that!"

"Does Elizabeth know how to write?"

"No . . . no . . . she just knows a few letters, but she will draw a picture." Littlefoot jumped from the saddle and ran to the short marker. Tossing aside the top two rocks, he carefully lifted the bottom one.

"Yes!" he shouted. "This is my mother's mark. Come and see! Come and see!"

Brannon rode toward the boy, leaned over in the saddle, and pulled off his hat so he could block the sun's bright morning rays. He squinted to see the etching in the desert floor.

I don't need eyeglasses, no matter what that Harriet Fletcher says. It's just . . . that . . . the sun seems brighter than normal. It must be the dry year we're having.

"Eh . . . is that an L . . . F . . . E?" he questioned.

"No, it's L - F - B. That's me!"

"You?"

"Yes, Littlefoot Brannon. My mother uses that as a sign for me!"

"Did she draw a picture? Is that a circle? What does a circle mean?"

"A circle means a lodge, a tepee . . . but this is not a circle because there are two little leaves and a stem on top."

"Stem? Leaves? Like an apple?"

"Or like an orange," Littlefoot added. "We saw an orange tree when we were in Florida."

"Well, there aren't any oranges anywhere out here, that's for sure . . . maybe it's a ball . . . or a bullet. There might be a wild plum somewhere near a river, and the old man mentioned peaches. Peaches! Littlefoot, she's gone to the peaches!"

"I thought you said they were all chopped down."

"Oh, those back up the canyon are gone, but the old man talked about peaches. Maybe there are more. Maybe she heard the Navajo talk about the peaches."

"But we don't know where they are," Littlefoot moaned.

"But we do know that this is her trail! We'll follow it as far as we can."

As it turned out, they followed the track the rest of the day and until noon the next day when it sloped down off the desert and led to a river that ran about six inches deep and twelve feet wide.

"Do you know where we are?" Littlefoot asked.

"Nope, but it must be somewhere in Utah. I've never heard of this stream in Arizona. I crossed this area in a sandstorm one time and found a stream like this. But I never really knew where I was. If this is the same stream, then we are no longer in Navajo territory. And if this stream runs in a dry year like this, it must run all the time, which means it just might be a good place to plant peaches."

"Do we go upstream or down?"

Brannon searched the horizon in both directions.

"Well, downstream puts us closer to those men on the mountain. They've got to be on our trail by now. So let's go upstream . . . at least for a while."

The stream led them on a gradual incline that broke off into deeper and deeper ravines. Finally the arroyos turned into small canyons, and the canyons grew large enough to support little patches of grass. They slowed their journey to let the horses graze and water.

"We have not seen any more markers," Littlefoot complained.

"Perhaps the animals knocked them over . . . or perhaps she did not feel well enough to get down and climb back on the pony. If she did go this way, she must have rode in the water, because we haven't see any sign all day."

It was twilight when they drew up at the mouth of a canyon that emptied a small, short waterfall into the main stream.

"There must be water and grass up there,"

Brannon pointed. "It will be a good place to camp for the night."

He turned Dos Vientos toward the mouth of the canyon. Suddenly a rifle shot kicked up dirt several feet in front of them. Brannon reached for his scabbard, then pulled his hand back.

"Stay on your horse!" he called to Littlefoot.

"They will kill us."

"No . . . from that range if they wanted us dead, they would have shot us easily the first time. It was just a warning."

"What kind of warning?"

"Do not enter."

"What are we going to do?"

"Enter, of course. Maybe they know where your mother is."

"Who is in there?"

"I don't know. Maybe that old prospector."

Brannon pulled off his hat and let it drop to his back, held on by the stampede string.

"Why did you take off your hat?"

"So they could see who it is."

"Do you think it is a friend who knows you?"

"Not necessarily, but I don't want to be mistaken for someone's enemy either."

As they proceeded, one more shot was fired in front of them. Brannon kept his gun in his holster and continued to ride into the canyon. Halfway through the mouth, three Indians, mounted on tall horses, came toward them with rifles pointed.

"Are they Navajo? The one in the red shirt

looks like he might be Navajo."

"They are Ute . . . Red Shirt?" he began. "Red Shirt! Is this the way you welcome Stuart Brannon to your camp?"

"The Brannon disguises himself as an old man without a boot. How did I know it was you?"

Brannon recognized the familiar melodious monotone. "It is no disguise. I am an old man without a boot," Brannon called. "It has been many years, my friend! What are you doing out in the canyons?"

"Those who dig for gold have chased us out of the mountains. It is a sad life. But we still have our peaches."

"Is this the canyon of the peaches?"

"Yes."

"Have you seen my mother?" Littlefoot shouted.

"I have seen many mothers."

"She is Nez Percé. She is riding alone. We think she is coming to . . ."

"She is with us, but she is very sick. We found her in the water of the stream three days ago. I do not think she will live long. She spoke like a crazy woman about The Brannon. Her body is weak, and her heart is broken because a disobedient son has run away from her!" Red Shirt scolded.

"I am the son! I am the disobedient son! I am back. She will get well now! I know she will get well! Where is she?"

"I will take you there. Are you being followed?"

"That might be. Seems like there's always someone trying to take a shot at me."

Red Shirt turned his horse and led Brannon and Littlefoot back into the canyon while the other two Indians remained out at the mouth.

Inside the steep walls of the canyon, Brannon came to fruit trees, picked clean, and leaves starting to turn yellow. The trees were scattered about in the canyon in no apparent order, but a small stream appeared to be flowing toward each one.

"Our camp is at the back. She is in my lodge. It is the big one in the middle."

"Red Shirt is the chief?" Brannon asked.

"Chief of a very small band." He watched the boy leap from his horse and run into the tent with pine trees crudely painted on the sides. Then turning to Brannon, Red Shirt warned, "She is very, very sick. She spits up much blood and sometimes cannot talk at all."

Brannon dismounted but did not enter the tent. One of the young men took his and Littlefoot's horses and turned them out in the trees. Brannon limped over toward the front flap of the tent.

"What happened to that foot?" Red Shirt asked.

"I lost my boot coming down a mountain."

"No, I meant what happened to that toe? It looks broken."

"I don't what to talk about it," Brannon insisted.

Littlefoot appeared at the door. Brannon could see tears streaming down his cheeks.

"She is sleeping, and I cannot wake her up!"

Brannon stooped through the deerhide doorway and stepped inside. The air was heavy with smoke from the campfire, and it was so dark that Brannon could barely make out a woman lying on a buffalo robe.

"We will make our camp outside by the trees," he told Red Shirt. Then he scooped up the woman, robe and all, and staggered out the door into the soft evening light.

He had taken about three steps when he glanced down at the woman in his arms. She was unconscious, but breathing. He studied her face.

Lord, Lord, is this Elizabeth? She looks so old . . . so tired . . . so fragile. God, You know the first time I picked her up and carried her — at Broken Arrow Crossing. She was beaten and bruised and freezing, but her body was young and strong. She weighs nothing now. She looks like she's fifty. Help her . . . help Littlefoot . . . help me!

He placed her near the base of one of the peach trees where the evening air blew fresh. Littlefoot knelt down beside her. Brannon turned away and wiped his eyes with the sleeve of his dirty shirt.

Expressionless, Red Shirt stood at his side.

It was several minutes before either man spoke.

"She has had a hard life," Red Shirt finally said.

"All she wanted was to go home to the Wallowas and raise her son in the land of her people," Brannon offered. "And they sent her off to Florida to catch a disease and die at the age of thirty."

"It is a story too often told," Red Shirt commented.

Brannon looked down at the frail body in the ragged brown government-issue dress.

"Red Shirt, I will ask you a big favor. Ask among your women if any will sell me a beaded deerskin dress, some moccasins, and a comb."

"You want them for her?"

"Yep."

"She might never wake up again."

"I'll pay a very good price," Brannon insisted.

"I will ask," Red Shirt agreed.

The sun was down behind the canyon wall, but there was still enough daylight to see when several Indian women brought a beautiful dress and moccasins to Brannon.

"Yes, I will buy those! Red Shirt, can you ask the women if they will wash her and put that new dress on her? I know she is unconscious, but if she wakes up, I want her to be wearing that deerskin."

He walked out among the trees and stared at

91

the canyon walls. The soil beneath his feet felt soft.

This is a good place to hide from the world. You can pretend that everything is different. Maybe we all need a hidden canyon.

When the women had finished, Brannon walked back over to the fire that Littlefoot had built near his mother and sat down on the buffalo robe next to her.

"Has she said anything?" he asked.

"No, she did not even awake when the women changed her clothing." Littlefoot looked around. "Where are the others?"

"They all went back to their lodges, I suppose. We'll wait for her to wake up."

"Yes, I will not rest all night!" Littlefoot pledged.

Within the hour, Littlefoot was asleep.

Brannon kept the fire going and cradled Elizabeth's head in his lap, combing her matted coarse black hair until it became smooth. He stared at the flames in the fire and relived the past twelve years of his life. It seemed like such a long time since he and the others had shared the little cabin at Broken Arrow Crossing. And yet he felt that that earlier kinship with the woman in his lap had never faded.

Lord, Elizabeth is like family . . . like a little sister. She moved away, but was always on my mind. I should have gone to Florida to look for her . . .

"Is The Brannon finished combing my hair?"

The weak voice seemed strangely magnified in the darkness of the night and startled his thoughts, sending chills down his back.

FIVE

"Eliza-Elizabeth!" Brannon stammered. Her head and shoulders seemed to take on a warmth he had not felt before.

"I knew you would come." Her voice was barely above a whisper. In the faint light of a dimly glowing fire, Brannon could see no more than a shadowy outline of her face.

"Did you know Littlefoot came after me?"

"Oh, he left without telling me because he was afraid I would not let him go, I suppose. He was right, of course. But I knew where he went. I knew he would find you. He is a brave warrior, you know."

"Yes . . . he is very much like his mother. But it is so dark. How did you know it was me?"

"The deerskin dress gave it away."

"The dress? But you can't even see it."

"Mr. Brannon, a woman never forgets the feel of soft deerskin. When I woke up, the first thing I felt was the deerskin. So I asked myself who would dress me in such a fine manner. And the only man who ever treated me with great respect came to mind. I knew you would come. Did you find my marker?"

"Yes. I suppose the Navajos were chased out of their camping place?"

"The Navajo wanted to go back to Window Rock, but I wanted to stay where you could find me, yet I did not want to get captured by the gunmen. The Navajo told me to camp with the Utes at the peaches, but I passed out before I got here . . ."

Brannon waited for her to continue. When she failed to speak, he nervously lifted her head to see her eyes.

"I am all right," she said. "I just need to rest sometimes."

"You rest all you want. I'll be right here."

"I know," she whispered and closed her eyes.

Brannon held her head in his lap and gazed at the other fires that flickered beside the Ute lodges.

Lord, that's what I miss — the campfires at night and the conversations of men. The stories . . . the wisdom . . . the laughter . . . even the stretchers. Everyone's too busy to sit around a fire anymore. That's what was missing at the ranch. We should have built a fire out in the yard. Earl, and Edwin, Peter, Doc, me and Tap, and the ladies, too, if they wanted.

Elizabeth shifted her weight, and he tried to make her more comfortable. After a moment, he sensed her eyes open so he glanced down.

"Do you feel like talking?" he asked.

"Yes."

"Elizabeth, this story about Littlefoot being my son? I don't understand. It doesn't sound

95

like the kind of lie that you would hang onto for so long."

"Does it offend you?"

"No, no, that's not it," he hurried to assure her.

"I have prayed often that my Jesus will forgive me. It was the desperate act of a desperate woman. May I have some water?"

Brannon gently laid her head on the buffalo robe. "Oh, yes, of course . . . and something to eat? Can you eat anything?"

"Perhaps some soft bread."

Within minutes Brannon had lifted her head and given her a drink. Then he sat back by her side and tore off some soft, inner chunks of bread and fed them to her a bite at a time.

He could see Elizabeth hold her sides when she coughed. After several minutes she began to talk again.

"Are we still in the camp of Red Shirt?" she asked.

"Yes. In the peach orchard."

"He is a true friend of The Brannon. He offered to take his whole band through Apache country and deliver me to your ranch."

Brannon nodded. "He would have done it, too."

"Yes, but I told him you would come. He knew you would also. He kept telling me not to die until The Brannon arrived."

"Well, I'm here . . . and I don't wan't you to die, do you hear?"

"I am glad."

"But what about Littlefoot?"

"You have not told him the truth?" Her voice sounded very tired.

"No, I didn't tell him anything . . . yet. But it was quite a shock to me and all my friends at the ranch when a son of mine showed up at the door. Did you think about the hardship that would have caused if I had married and had my own family?" he pressed.

"I knew you would not marry," she whispered. "You did not put this dress on me either, did you?"

"Eh . . . no, the ladies did that."

"I don't believe the years have changed you much."

"Just wait until daylight. You will find it is an old man who visits with you."

"I do not believe that."

"Well, as I was sayin' . . . eh . . . what about this big stretcher about me being Littlefoot's father?"

She folded her thin hands on her stomach and took as deep a breath as she dared. "I would like to sit up."

Brannon slowly lifted her up and kept one arm around her frail shoulders.

"When we arrived in Oklahoma after the surrender at Bear Paw . . ." She spoke in labored, choppy spurts. "We were mixed in with other peoples. They began to call my son a breed. They were very angry at the white men and anyone who had been friendly with them.

97

So Littlefoot and I were treated harshly.

"When he got old enough, he began to question why he was called a breed and wanted to know about his father. I just did not know how to tell him his father bought, beat, abused, abandoned, and tried to kill me. He needed something better than that. We both needed hope."

Elizabeth took several deep breaths, clutched her sides, and leaned against Brannon's chest.

"So one wretched day I invented the story that his father was The Brannon. It helped him to feel important. After a while, I began to enjoy the lie also. I kept telling him that you would be worried sick about us and try to find us. Over the years, after we were moved to Florida . . . we had almost given up hope. I got very sick and was afraid we would both die in the swamps.

"But when your letters came . . . it proved to Littlefoot that his father . . . The Brannon . . . had been searching for him all these years. He insisted that we take the money you sent in one of the letters and come to you. But as you can see . . . the journey has been difficult for me."

"You are very sick. You shouldn't have tried such a journey."

"I am dying. But I would rather die in the mountains than in the swamps. Did you find gold in the mountains above Broken Arrow Crossing?"

"Well . . . sort of . . . I mean, we found some gold, but it's a very long story."

"Tell me the real stories of The Brannon," she pleaded. "Littlefoot has read me the books, but they do not sound like The Brannon I know."

As Elizabeth drifted in and out of sleep, he told her about the Little Stephen Mine, about marshaling in Tres Casas, about the further conflict with Rutherfords in Paradise Meadow, about returning to the ranch, and the Yavapai County War. He told her about driving cattle out of Mexico and about Señora Pacifica.

As the sky was turning from black to gray, she woke up in a deep sweat, and Brannon washed her face with a clean bandanna.

"It is almost morning," she whispered. "I rejoice in each one. Someday soon I will see my last morning."

"Don't talk that way. Many folks find the desert is good for coughing sickness," Brannon scolded.

"Yes, if I could have come out here a few years ago, it could have changed things. Not now. It is too late."

"We need to talk about Littlefoot," Brannon urged. "Soon it will be daylight, and he will wake up."

"Will you take him to live on your ranch?" she asked.

"Of course. You knew I would do that."

"Yes." She paused to cough and clutch her side. "Yes, I knew you would. He is a good worker. He will not be a bother. He will keep up with the other workers."

"Elizabeth, Littlefoot will not come to my house as a worker. He will live with me in the big house, and I will look after him like . . . like an uncle. But you will come and live with me also."

"I do not think I will live that long."

"We'll let the Lord decide on that."

"Yes . . . yes, I am in His hands."

"But what about Littlefoot? We must tell him the truth."

"Yes, it is time. I will tell him when he awakes."

"I'll help you talk to him if you like."

"No, it is something I must do myself. Perhaps if you were not here, it would be better."

"Well I'll . . . eh, go . . . eh, check on the horses and rig up a travois for you to ride. Are you going to be all right? You were in pretty bad shape yesterday."

"I have Littlefoot and you to look after me. That is twice what I had yesterday. I believe I shall not die today."

At daybreak Brannon rode out of the canyon to the river. Wearing a pair of moccasins and an old deerhide shirt he had wrangled from Red Shirt, he slipped off Dos Vientos and climbed some rocks. He searched the landscape several miles downstream.

The morning air felt good in his lungs, and

he took deep breaths, savoring the vitality. The sound of running water was faint, but steady — reminding him of life barely hanging on through a rough autumn draught. The beef jerky that he chewed had no flavor except for the salt and spices with which it was cured.

He glanced back to see Red Shirt ride up on his sorrel stallion.

"There will be no rain," his Ute friend reported.

"Nope," Brannon replied as he glanced at the blue, cloudless sky.

"You will be leaving today?" Red Shirt asked.

"Yep, Elizabeth seems a little better. I want to travois her until I can get a wagon. I'm taking her to my ranch."

"They are leaving today also," Red Shirt announced, waving his arms at the lodges around him.

"Leaving? Don't you spend the winter here?"

"No. We will go back to the other canyons. You have many men following you, and we do not want them to find our peaches."

Brannon jerked around. "Following me? Are they coming this way?"

"They have turned downstream, but will come back this way in a day or so. I will tell my people to go downstream to the green trees, then head north into the canyons. Those that follow you will see the tracks and perhaps not come this far up the river."

Brannon looked over at Red Shirt. His back

was straight, his shoulders wide, his muscles tight.

"What do you mean — tell your people? Aren't you going with them?"

"I will go with The Brannon until he can trade for a wagon."

"You should stay with your people. It is safer for you," Brannon insisted.

"And The Brannon should have stayed with his people. We do not always do the safe thing, do we?"

Brannon remounted Dos Vientos. He offered Red Shirt some jerky, and the Indian traded him a dried peach. Riding downstream for several miles, neither man spoke.

Lord, if this was fifty years ago, back when Walker, Smith, Carson, Meek, and the others were the only ones in the mountains, I would have just camped with Red Shirt for the winter. Hang a little meat, bundle up some plews, chop some firewood, tell a few stories around the fire. Sometimes, Lord, sometimes I feel like a man born untimely late.

"My people will turn there!" Red Shirt pointed to a trail winding up the river bank and across the desert into southeastern Utah Territory. At that point, both men circled their horses and began to ride back to the canyon of the peaches.

"Do you know how far until we get to a town or stage stop?" Brannon asked.

"Two and a half, maybe three days. We will

stay on the side of the river all the way," Red Shirt reported. "Why do the angry men follow The Brannon?"

"To kill me, I reckon. I think one of them might be an old enemy from the days up on the Plata. Do you remember those days?"

"I remember that The Brannon would give food to some very hungry Utes. And I remember a man who tried to steal your hole in the mountain. Perhaps the old way is better."

"The old way?" Brannon quizzed.

"Either make friends with your enemies, or kill them. That way you do not always have to keep looking over your shoulder."

Brannon admired the sincerity in Red Shirt's bronzed face and deep, dark eyes.

"There are times when I surely agree with you," Brannon finally admitted. "But we'll have to all give account to a Higher Power than ourselves. And the Good Book says we should try to learn to love our enemies."

"The Brannon's God has smiled on him. But others, like the Nez Percé woman . . . He seems to ignore. Perhaps this Jesus is only God for white people?"

"Red Shirt, if there's one thing I know, it's that the Lord doesn't give a cow chip what your color is. He looks at a man's heart. And it's in a man's heart that he has to believe."

"Elizabeth believes," Red Shirt continued. "She told us so."

"Well, belief doesn't mean an easy life . . . it

means help through all the struggles of this life. And a future life a whole lot better than this one."

"You mean Heaven?" Red Shirt asked.

"Yep."

"I like the stories of Heaven," Red Shirt admitted. "I think I should — " He stopped in mid-sentence and pointed upstream. "Is the boy looking for you?"

Littlefoot was riding Six Bits straight across the stream, up the steep embankment, and into the desert.

"No . . . I don't think so. He knows where we are. I think he just found out that I'm not his father."

"Will you ride after him?"

"No . . . if his mother told him about his real father, I think he'll need some time to beat on the sagebrush and scream in his heart."

The deep leathery creases turned up at the sides of Red Shirt's mouth as he smiled. "The Brannon speaks like a man who has spent some days beating on the sage and screaming in his heart. Perhaps The Brannon has some Indian blood in him?"

"Yes . . . perhaps . . . or perhaps all men hurt the same."

Red Shirt started to say something, then caught himself, and returned to his usual emotionless gaze. As they rode back into the peach grove canyon, Brannon was surprised to find every lodge taken down. Everyone scurried to break camp. He rode straight to Elizabeth who was being given some water by an attractive young Ute woman.

"She is the one who sold you the dress," Red Shirt announced.

Brannon eased himself out of the saddle and dropped Dos Vientos's reins to the ground. The big horse grazed out toward the trees. Then looking at the young woman, Brannon gave her a brief nod. "Thanks for helping Elizabeth. And for the dress and moccasins."

The young woman would not look him in the eyes, but kept her head bowed. "I have heard often Red Shirt's stories of his friend, The Brannon. I am happy to help such a brave man." She turned and left him with Elizabeth.

"Red Shirt's a good man," he told Elizabeth. "And his daughter seems to be very polite."

A smile flashed across Elizabeth's face, momentarily taking ten years off her looks. "His daughter? That is his wife!"

"His wife? But she's so . . . young."

"She is older than I was when Littlefoot was born," Elizabeth informed him. "Perhaps The Brannon is getting senile?"

He brushed his gray-streaked hair back over his ears. "Yeah . . . that's what folks keep telling me."

"You have nothing to hide," she said. "And you have seen me ugly before. Only last time it was with bruises, not age. I do not look in the mirror anymore. It always makes me cry. I was pretty once; do you remember?"

Brannon glanced away from Elizabeth.

"Yes," he choked, wiping his eyes with the back of his hand. "I remember."

Brannon didn't dare turn back for several minutes. Instead, he helped Red Shirt lash travois poles to his saddle. When the stretcher was secure, he dragged it over to her and stepped to her side.

"When will Littlefoot be back?" he asked.

"When he has run out of tears," she answered.

"He is angry, I suppose."

"Yes."

Brannon pulled off his black hat and held it in his hand. "At me, or at you?"

"Both of us. It is very difficult for a young boy to go through this."

"And it is very difficult for his mother. Did you tell him how his real father died?"

She looked Brannon in the eyes. "Yes. He pleaded to know. I had to tell him. I told him how you saved our lives."

"Did you tell him that I was serious about you two living with me? Did you tell him you are like family to a man with no family?"

"I told him that."

"What did he say?"

"He said . . ." Elizabeth paused and looked away.

"What did he say?" Brannon asked again.

"He said . . . that he would avenge his father's death. He is just a hurting boy. He will come back with a clear mind," she assured him.

By midmorning the band of Utes had left the peach canyon, and only Brannon, Red Shirt, and Elizabeth were left. She slept on the buffalo robe while the two men sat and drank coffee at the fire.

"Do you want me to go and look for the boy?" Red Shirt asked.

"If he's not back when the sun is high, we will all go and look for him."

"He wants to kill you?"

"He wants to make someone hurt for all his pain. I make a good target," Brannon suggested. He stood and walked back toward the peach trees and gazed toward the far end of the canyon. "Red Shirt, I never noticed those diggin's back in the canyon. With all the lodges up, I couldn't see the holes. Is there gold back there?"

Red Shirt shrugged. "I do not think so. Years ago the Navajo planted these trees. They said they got them from black-robed priests. When the troops made the Navajo stay to the south, they had to abandon this canyon. But one of my sisters married a Navajo, and he had been here as a boy. So now it is ours. When we came, those holes were dug, but we have never seen anyone here. I do not know who dug them, but I suppose if there had been gold, he would have returned."

"Unless he got killed . . . or lost. I met an old man who told me about gold in the peaches, but he was sort of desert-crazy. I didn't know whether to believe him or not. Why don't your people dig for the gold?"

"For what purpose? If we find gold, the troops will come and take away the land. We would lose both the gold and the fruit trees. This way we at least have the peaches. Here comes the boy."

Brannon turned to watch Littlefoot gallop up the canyon on the pinto.

"There are riders down on the river!" he shouted.

"How far down?"

"Beyond the place where the Utes turned north."

"We should leave this canyon," Brannon advised.

Elizabeth pushed herself up on an elbow and called to Littlefoot. "Did the desert help you think of my words more clearly?" she asked.

"Yes. Now I know what I must do." Turning to Brannon, he announced, "I will avenge my real father's death. I will kill his slayer. Then I will ride into the canyons and live with the Utes."

"Littlefoot!" his mother called.

"The one who murders The Brannon will not be welcome among the Utes," Red Shirt warned.

"Then I will go to the Navajo. It does not matter."

Brannon walked over to Dos Vientos and

pulled his shotgun out of the center of his bedroll. Reaching into his saddlebag, he scooped out two shells and cracked the gun, filling both cylinders. Snapping the gun closed, he walked back over to Littlefoot who stood, slightly trembling, next to his mother.

"Now, son, let's get — "

"I am not your son!" the boy replied roughly.

"No, you aren't my son. My son died at birth a year before you were born. He never had a chance to know his mother or his father. He never rode a pinto horse, or swam in fresh water, or ate homemade tortillas. He never laughed at his mother's jokes, nor watched his father quiet a snuffy horse. But if my son had been allowed to grow up, I reckon he'd be a lot like you. He'd be a little brave and a little smart, and a whole lot stubborn. Now here's the gun." Brannon shoved the shotgun into Littlefoot's hands. I'm going to stand about ten foot back here so you can't miss. Now you go right ahead and pull that trigger. I mean it. If you're goin' to shoot me, shoot me right now. Because I'm not about to spend the rest of my days knowing that Elizabeth's son wants to kill me. That would break my heart and blur the fine memories I have of your mother. Do it right now, or I don't ever want you to talk that way again!"

Littlefoot lifted the gun to his shoulder and pointed it at Brannon's chest.

There was a long pause.

Brannon felt the slight breeze of the canyon; the sky reflected another cloudless day; the air was fresh. It was a beautiful day, marred by the bizarre sight of a young boy propping up a heavy, shaking gun.

Lord, I would rather this not be my last day on earth.

Then Littlefoot threw the gun to the ground, dropped to his knees, and began to cry. Elizabeth struggled to get up out of the stretcher on the travois, but Red Shirt put a hand on her shoulder and held her back.

Brannon walked over to the boy, knelt down beside him, and threw his arms around Littlefoot. The boy continued to sob, and Brannon held him tight.

Several minutes later Red Shirt announced, "We should leave the canyon before the others find us here."

Littlefoot held on to Brannon. "If I lose my mother, I will have no one!" he cried.

"Those letters I sent over the years were not lies. I meant every word. I have wanted you two to come live at my home for years. When I left my ranch last week, it was not a game. I came here because I am very concerned about my good friend Elizabeth and her son. She told you the truth about the fight I had with your real father. I had to choose quickly whether to save your mother's life and yours . . . or his. And I chose to save yours. I do not regret that decision in the least. Now I'm askin' you, man to man, will you and your mother please come and live at my ranch?"

Littlefoot stood up and walked over to his mother's side. He laid his head on her shoulder, and she reached up and wiped his eyes with her hand.

"Mother," he sobbed, "why couldn't The Brannon have been my real father?"

"That is one of the first questions I intend to ask my Jesus," she whispered.

Red Shirt led the procession out of the canyon. Then came Brannon, pulling the travois, with Elizabeth resting on the stretcher. Littlefoot rode the pinto by his mother's side.

He carried the loaded shotgun across his lap.

SIX

Stuart Brannon scanned the small procession as they rode out of the canyon and started down the river. Littlefoot . . . rough brown shirt, duckings, suspenders, and dark shock of thick hair . . . sitting tall on the pinto, displaying his regal Nez Percé heritage.

Red Shirt . . . red flannel shirt, felt hat pulled low . . . skin deep brown and rawhide tough . . . always stoic, cautious . . . surveying the countryside for miles in every direction.

Elizabeth, wrapped in hides, with only head and arms showing, lay on her back on the stretcher, dragged over the riverbank on the travois . . . her eyes tight, drawn, tired . . . her hair recently combed smooth, but generally without direction and starting to gray. Her face was protected from the dust with Brannon's bandanna. Under the blanket, lying on her beaded deerskin dress and clutched in her hands, was his Bible.

She didn't complain.

She never complained.

Lord, look at us here. Me with this buckskin shirt and moccasins, eagle feather in my hat . . . anybody would think we're just an Indian family on the move. Maybe that's what we are. Lord, maybe this is my family.

The slight breeze from the west now felt pleasant, but Brannon knew it would grow warm as the day progressed. He sat up in the saddle and took a deep breath. There was a faint hint of change in what he tasted in his lungs. It was something more than the pungent aroma of scattered sagebrush. Exploring the horizon to the west, he saw nothing but blue sky and distant mountains.

"Do you smell that?" he called back to Red Shirt.

Waving his arms to the sky, Red Shirt observed, "I think maybe it will rain . . . in two days."

"I think you're right." Then he glanced down at Elizabeth. Her eyes were closed.

Maybe we should just ride north . . . up to the canyons . . . up to the mountains . . . up to Oregon and the Wallowas . . . Maybe I should have stuck with her in the —

"Look!" Littlefoot shouted, across the river to the left. "There are riders!"

Brannon squinted his eyes at the south. The sun was blazing, and the reflection was bright. His eyes felt dry and strained. He couldn't see anything unusual.

"There are three of them," Red Shirt called out. "Are they some of those The Brannon was expecting to follow him?"

Brannon stood in the stirrups, pulled his hat

lower, and searched the horizon, still seeing nothing.

"They've spotted us and are riding this way," Littlefoot cautioned. "Will we try to outrun them?"

Finally Brannon caught sight of the dust and could locate the riders.

"The only place to run would be back to peach canyon," he reported. "So let's just keep our pace and see what happens."

"If we run, it will show we are afraid," Red Shirt cautioned. "We have three warriors and a brave Nez Percé woman. There is no reason to run."

"Let's continue on our gait and act like we're ignoring them. Red Shirt, if they ride up here, you do the talking."

"Well, keep your hat low," Red Shirt warned. "If they see the white at the top of your forehead, they won't think much of your Indian blood."

"Littlefoot, lay that shotgun so that it's facing them as they ride up," Brannon advised.

"I would like to carry a gun also," Elizabeth called out.

Brannon hauled a spare Colt out of his saddlebag, pulled five bullets out of his belt, and loaded the chambers. Then he climbed down off Dos Vientos and handed the worn, wooden-handled revolver to Elizabeth.

"Now I don't plan on you needin' to use this," Brannon tried to assure her.

"No. I do not plan on it either. But," she added, "I will defend my family."

Lord, it's the only family she has . . . too.

As the riders drew closer, Brannon and the others continued on their way. The three riders splashed through the river and raced closer.

"Do you want me to go out and talk to them?" Red Shirt asked.

"Let them make the first play. If they want a fight, you take the one on the left; I'll take the one on the sorrel, and Littlefoot can aim at the middle. But let's see if we can ride out of this without shooting."

Just before the three men caught up, Brannon led the party up on a rise next to the river, which gave them a height advantage over the pursuing gunmen. It was the man on the sorrel horse who reached them first and hollered out to Littlefoot, who was still leading the procession.

"Boy, I want to talk to you!"

Brannon kept his head down, his hat pulled low, and his finger on the trigger of the cocked Winchester.

Red Shirt rode up to the man.

"The boy does not understand," Red Shirt offered. "What do you want?"

"That boy was riding that pinto with a white man named Stuart Brannon. We're looking for him, and I want the boy to tell me where he's at," the man demanded.

"I will ask him," Red Shirt replied.

Brannon noticed that all the while Red Shirt

asked Littlefoot a question in Ute, he never took his eye off the men, but kept his rifle pointed in their direction.

Red Shirt's talkin' Ute, and Littlefoot's answerin' in Nez Percé. They don't know what the other's sayin', but it doesn't matter 'cause this old boy can't tell the difference!

"He says . . . the man he was riding with is now on his way back to his ranch," Red Shirt reported.

"When did he start out?" the gunman demanded.

"Early this morning."

"What direction did he take?"

Brannon kept peeking from under his hat at the man in the middle. He had a deep scar across the back of his right hand and a reddish-gray beard that looked about a week old.

After further contrived conversation, Red Shirt continued, "He says the man headed west when he rode out of camp."

"West?" the man shouted. "You four are headed west! Joey, these Injuns don't know directions at all!"

"The boy's lyin'," Joey growled. "Shoot that one on the black horse, and maybe the boy's memory will return." He nodded at Brannon.

"Shoot him?" the man asked. "I ain't goin' around shootin' Injuns in cold blood. No, sir, not unless there's a reward or somethin' . . . Trevor said just to question 'em and then hightail it back to camp."

Joey whipped out his revolver, only to find Brannon's Winchester pointed at his head and Littlefoot's shotgun aimed at his midsection.

"Drop it," Brannon barked, "or you won't have enough parts left to send home to mama!"

"Who are you?" Joey gasped, obviously startled to discover Brannon wasn't an Indian.

The other two men started to draw their guns, but Red Shirt covered one, and Littlefoot turned his attention to the other.

"I'm the man you never want to meet up with in the desert."

"He's The Brannon!" Littlefoot reported.

"That ain't Brannon," one man grumbled. "I seen him once in Mexico. Brannon's got sandy-colored hair."

"And he's a bigger man."

"Now you boys can believe anything you want, but unless you holster those guns, you're going to be laying on this desert with buzzards flockin' around you," Brannon warned.

Both outside gunmen slipped their revolvers back into their holsters. Joey didn't flinch.

"Come on, Joey . . . we can wait a while to collect that money," one muttered.

"There's more to this than money!"

"Not for me, there ain't. Lonnie, you comin' with me?"

Brannon never took his eyes off the one called Joey.

"Joey! Don't be a pig-headed fool! There'll be

another day. We'll ride back for the others and make our play later."

"We bring him in, boys, and we'll be rich! Lonnie, you shoot the boy. I'll take Brannon down, and Slim can drop the one in the red shirt."

In the silence of the standoff the click of Elizabeth's revolver being cocked riveted their attention.

"The squaw's got a gun, too!" one of the men shouted.

"Joey-man," Elizabeth called out, "I do not think I like you!" She raised the gun and pointed it at him.

He swung his shoulders and gun toward her to shoot. At that instant Brannon fired a shot that struck the man in the arm between the shoulder and the elbow. The man tumbled out of the saddle onto the ground, dropping his revolver.

One gunman turned his horse and spurred it in retreat. The other threw up his hands and cried, "Don't shoot! Oh, please, Brannon, I've got a wife and kids at home!"

"Get out of here!" Brannon shouted as he jumped off Dos Vientos and ran toward Joey, who grabbed his ragged bleeding arm.

"Lonnie, don't leave me!"

"It was a dumb play, Joey. I ain't ridin' with no fools like that! Don't shoot, Mister! I'm leavin'! Don't let them Injuns shoot me in the back!" he hollered as he spurred his horse to catch up with the fleeing gunman.

"Brannon," Joey pleaded, "tie my belt on this arm . . . I'm going to bleed to death!"

Kicking the man's discarded revolver out of reach, Brannon pulled his folding knife out of his pocket and cut a short piece of saddle string off Joey's rigging. He yanked it hard around the wounded man's upper arm, then tugged off Joey's bandanna, and wrapped it around the wound.

"Trevor will get you, Brannon," he snarled. "You know he will get you!"

"I think I will shoot this man," Red Shirt announced. "He must be the stupidest man on earth."

Red Shirt raised his rifle and pointed it at the man's head.

"He's jokin', ain't he, Brannon?" the man choked.

"Wait a minute!" Brannon called to Red Shirt, waving his hand. "Let me move away from here. I don't want blood sprayin' all over this new shirt."

"Wait! Wait! Give me a chance!" the man cried. "I'll ride out of here. I'll head north and never look back. No, sir . . . how about it?"

"I don't know how long I can keep this wild Ute from leadin' you down," Brannon snarled. "So you better mount up and make a run for it."

The wounded man pulled himself up on his horse and turned it north. "My gun! I got to have my gun!"

"Dead men don't need a Colt," Brannon counseled.

With that the man kicked his horse and galloped north. As the dust trailed away from them, Littlefoot rode over to Brannon.

"Why didn't you shoot him?" he asked.

"Shoot him?" Brannon questioned. "I did shoot him!"

"I mean, why didn't you kill him? He was going to shoot my mother."

"I stopped him from tryin' something dumb, but after that I couldn't see pluggin' him again."

"The Brannon took a chance shooting him in the arm," Red Shirt added. "I would have shot him in the stomach."

"The Brannon is a very good shot, you know," Littlefoot bragged.

"I'm mighty lucky; that's what I am. I aimed to hit him in the chest, but he jerked around with that gun, and I clipped his arm. I almost missed him completely. I had no intention of winging him."

"What happens now?" Elizabeth asked.

"I suppose they'll go back and report to Trevor. I would expect the whole bunch to be on our tail by tomorrow," Brannon reported.

"Do you think that one will keep riding north?" Littlefoot asked.

"Yep. Most men don't have a heart for killin'. Oh, they can brag about it in a saloon or around a campfire, but it just isn't in them. They'll ride out here and shoot at us as long as they think they won't take a slug. Trevor's the bad one. If he's made up his mind to kill me, then he will."

"What?" Littlefoot demanded.

"He'll either kill me, or die tryin'."

"So . . . what does The Brannon do from here?" Red Shirt asked.

"Well, I'm still goin' home. But we might have to make a stand against this bunch, so I reckon we should circle up to the north and ride beside the canyons. It will be longer, but there's more protection."

"Perhaps The Brannon would like to ride nights and rest days?" Red Shirt asked.

"Now that's a powerful good idea. We'll keep goin' today and tonight, and then we'll sleep up in those hills in the morning. That just might give us a jump on them." Then he turned back to Elizabeth. She had propped herself up on her elbow and begun to cough.

"You feel like making a long journey today?" Brannon inquired.

Gasping for a breath, she finally answered, "I feel like closing my eyes and sleeping forever."

"We'll stop right here," Brannon decided.

"Mr. Brannon . . . I intend to see the shade of your home, and you know I can be a very stubborn person. We will go on," she overruled.

Dragging the travois made the journey extremely slow. Brannon spent most of the day wiping sweat from his brow, giving Elizabeth a drink, and looking back over his shoulder.

Red Shirt rode ahead of them to find a trail along the rocky canyon walls. Littlefoot spent most of the time riding within view of his mother.

"She is sleeping now," he reported.

"That's good." Brannon nodded.

"Do you pray for my mother to get well?" he asked.

"Yep."

"Well, why doesn't her God heal her?"

"Son . . . I wish I had a good answer for you. But I do know that God doesn't jump when we shout. He is not a horse with us holding the reins. In fact, it's just the opposite. He is in control, and we have to assume He's leading in a good and perfect way."

"My mother does not pray for healing any more. I have heard her pray in Nez Percé. She wants to go home to her Jesus."

"Your mother hurts very much. She longs to go to a place where there is no pain," Brannon explained.

"Well, it seems to me that she would rather be with her Jesus than with me."

Brannon stared over at the dark eyes that waited for wisdom. He searched the horizon, hoping for a diversion.

None came.

"Why does my mother want to leave me?" Littlefoot asked again.

"Son, your mother . . . she has thought about you, loved you, worked for you her whole life. From the day you were born . . . and remember, I was there . . . from that day on you have been the center of her thoughts and actions. But your mother knows what is happening. She will not be able to raise you much longer . . . she will not see you grow up, get married, raise a fine family, and have a life of your own. She hurts because of all the things she will never see. But if she only thought about the sadness, her heart would break, and she would die even faster. So in order to survive, she thinks about Heaven. It gives her a peace in her heart, and she can face each day a little better. Don't get mad at her for wishing to be with the Lord. Son, you remember, for the rest of your life there will never be a person on this earth that could ever love you more than your mama."

Littlefoot brushed back the tears from his eyes.

"Now you ride on up there and see if you can find Red Shirt," Brannon suggested.

Littlefoot galloped ahead of the slow-moving travois. As soon as his hoofbeats receded, Elizabeth called out. Brannon stopped Dos Vientos, grabbed his canteen, and slid out of the saddle. He drooped the reins over the horn and walked to her side, propped up her head, and helped her drink. Holding her weak shoulders, he noticed tears streaking across her face.

"Is there a lot of pain?" Brannon asked.

"Those are joyful tears." She tried to smile. "I have listened to you talk to Littlefoot. You were speaking my heart to my son, and I am grateful."

"Eh . . . well, I . . . I didn't know what to say, actually. It's just . . ."

"I must make a request of you."

"You just name it."

"Will you assure me that you will not let my son marry a nonbeliever?"

"What?"

"He must marry a Christian."

"Oh . . . well, I . . . I don't know if I can make —"

"Please . . . I must know that much at least," she pleaded.

"Listen," Brannon insisted, "you get down to my ranch, and that desert air will make you feel so good you'll live until Littlefoot is an old man."

"The Brannon does not lie very good. You haven't had much practice at it. Will you make me that promise?"

"I promise to insist that he follows his mother's wishes," Brannon agreed.

"Yes . . . yes . . . that is all you can do. Mr. Brannon, I can never repay you for all the kindness you have shown me and Littlefoot. I pray that our God will give you the desires of your heart. You deserve them."

Brannon wiped her forehead with a wet bandanna, then mounted Dos Vientos, and continued the journey.

The desires of my heart? The desire of my heart was for Lisa to live! Lord, the desire of my heart is to love my wife, spend my days raising my son . . . and looking into the eyes of my grandchildren! Lord, the desires of my heart . . . the desires of my heart are buried under the piñons on a hill next to Sunrise Creek.

They plodded across the desert into the hills and down a narrow mountain trail. They tramped along through sunset, supper, and under the stars. It was Brannon's intention to ride all night, rest during the day, and ride into Medicine Hat, Utah, the next evening.

But at midnight the plans changed.

"I think my mother's very sick," Littlefoot called as they stopped to rest the horses. "She doesn't want to wake up!"

Brannon limped over to her side. Quickly he pulled the bandanna away from her face and bent over to listen to her breathing.

"Her lungs are filling up! We've got to get her to sit up and cough that out. Red Shirt, we'll make camp right here."

"It is not a good place to defend," the Indian replied.

"We have no choice. Picket the horses and watch the trail behind us," Brannon commanded. "Littlefoot, build a fire. We'll need some water boiling!"

They hurried about their tasks with their only light a quarter moon that gave the mountain a purple-black reflection. The air cooled, and Brannon noticed an occasional cloud floating its shadow across the campsite. In the distance he heard a single coyote howl at the night. The fire crackled as he dug a sack out of his bedroll.

He laid Elizabeth on the buffalo robe stretched across the ground, and he propped her up against a stack of saddles. Littlefoot huddled over his mother.

"She is very warm!"

"Keep that cool rag on her forehead," Brannon ordered.

"She keeps calling out for her Jesus, but she won't talk to me," Littlefoot complained.

"She's delirious. She's not thinking right now, son . . . you just keep her cool while I get this water boiling."

"What are you going to do with it?"

"We'll . . . we'll make a steam tent and try to get her to inhale some of these camphor fumes." He pointed at the little cork-stopped, green bottle that he held in his hand.

"Will that make her well?"

"It might help clear up her lungs for a little while . . . that's all we can hope."

"Is she going to die this time?" Littlefoot asked.

Brannon stared at the boy and then at Elizabeth. He opened his mouth, but no words came out. Then he turned back to the fire and the pot of boiling water.

"Help me bring her over to the fire," he requested. He slipped one arm under Elizabeth and put another behind her head.

Lord, she doesn't weigh seventy-five pounds! There's nothing left. She can't keep this up . . . she'll never live to see . . .

"What do you want now?" Littlefoot asked.

"You hold her up. If she comes to, try to get her to cough."

Brannon soaked a clean bandanna with the camphor and then laid the cloth over the pot of boiling water. Next he fashioned a small tent out of his saddle blanket and captured the camphor fumes in the point of the blanket.

With Littlefoot's help, they positioned Elizabeth under the blanket and into the mist of camphor steam. Within a few moments she began to cough.

And cough.

And cough.

Finally Brannon pulled the saddle blanket tent back away from her face and held both shoulders tight so she had to remain upright.

"Keep wiping her forehead with the cool water," he ordered.

"She is sweating all over," Littlefoot reported.

"Yeah . . . it's like a bad fever . . . a very bad fever. She was coughing up blood, wasn't she?"

"Yes," Littlefoot answered. "I don't think she can go on like this very long."

Elizabeth began to gasp for breath. Her eyes

opened wide, and she stared at Brannon.

"Elizabeth?" he whispered.

There was a long pause. "Yes?" she panted.

"You had a bad spell . . . we were worried." Brannon's voice faltered, but he kept his grip on her. "I would lay you down, but it might be easier to breathe sitting up."

"Yes," she whispered. "Hold me up . . . keep holding me."

"Mother," Littlefoot moaned, "you kept calling for your Jesus. I thought . . . I thought you were . . ." He couldn't force himself to complete the sentence.

"I didn't know that I called out to Jesus, but I could have . . . He's the only one I could call to at such a time."

Littlefoot continued to hold her hand. "Mother, I was very worried."

"Was The Brannon worried?" she asked her son.

"He is never worried." Littlefoot shrugged.

"You are wrong," she sighed. "Do not be anxious about me until you see The Brannon worried. I am all right now. We should ride on farther."

"You need the rest," Brannon insisted.

"This is not a very safe-looking camp," she offered.

"We are not riding on. We will sit right here until you are stronger."

"You are very stubborn." She offered a smile that came out more like a grimace.

"So I've been told. Would you like to try and eat anything?"

"Perhaps I can drink some water," she sighed.

Through the rest of the night Brannon and Red Shirt took turns standing guard along the trail. Littlefoot never left his mother's side. At daylight Red Shirt came back from the lookout and sat down cross-legged next to Brannon.

"Will we ride today?"

"I don't think she's up to it." Brannon motioned to the sleeping Elizabeth.

"Do you think they are following us?"

"Yep."

"Then they will catch us today."

"That would be my guess."

Red Shirt continued, "We should find better cover. Even The Brannon cannot hide in this clearing."

"You ride up the trail and find us some protection. We'll follow as soon as they stir around."

Red Shirt began to saddle his horse. Then he turned back and ran his fingers through his thick black hair. "Why does The Brannon do all of this for a dying woman who is not one of his people?"

"Because, well . . . we are friends . . . and she *is* one of 'my' people. You know . . . a man's got to do what's right."

"And who tells The Brannon what is right?"

"Why . . . it's just right . . . I mean . . . it's what God wants me to do, that's all."

"I like this God of yours. Is He the Jesus that the Nez Percé calls for in the night?"

"Yeah . . . that's the one."

Red Shirt mounted his horse and turned to the trail. Then he rode back by the campfire. "One day The Brannon should come and visit my lodge and tell us more about his Jesus."

"That's a promise you can count on."

"Yes, yes, The Brannon has promised. It will be done."

Within an hour Brannon, Littlefoot, and Elizabeth were on the trail, following Red Shirt up into the barren desert hills. Before midmorning they were once again unpacking, this time in the shadow of a shallow cave that had for a few days been the object of some miner's dream.

"He gave up before he got to bedrock," Brannon observed as he studied the diggings.

"Maybe he discovered no gold," Littlefoot replied. "What do we do now?"

Brannon organized the defense.

"You stay at the cave with Elizabeth. Your job is to protect your mother."

"What will I do if they come after us?" the boy asked.

"You are a brave warrior . . . you will know what to do." Brannon nodded at Elizabeth. "Right, mother?"

"Yes, he is a brave warrior like his grandfather. He will know."

Brannon secured the horses behind the boulders, pulled out his rifle, and stuffed his pockets with extra cartridges. He and Red Shirt took up positions fifty feet downhill from the diggings.

With rifle in hand and hat pulled down tight, Brannon sat in the hot desert sun and waited for any sign of riders.

"Will we shoot them all?" Red Shirt asked.

"No . . . no, we'll try to get them to ride on. 'Course Trevor won't likely want to ride."

"Then we shall kill him."

Brannon calculated Red Shirt's determination.

"Listen, we are almost to Medicine Hat. Maybe you should ride on up to your family now. No reason for you to —"

"No, I will not leave."

"It's not your battle," Brannon reminded him.

"It's not The Brannon's battle either. I will stay. How many fights do you think I have left? They want us to sit in our lodges and eat the corn that our animals refuse to touch. I would rather be in the hills with The Brannon."

"We might not win this battle."

"Then Red Shirt will become part of the legends told around the campfires of my people. There are worse things than dying."

"Yeah . . . I think I've said that a time or two. Look, if they ride up here, wait for them to come into range, and then shoot every horse in sight."

"Horses?" Red Shirt questioned.

"I want every man to know that this is where we draw the line. They'd better decide whether they really want to fight. This is not some boy's game."

"And what do we do until they catch up with us."

"We wait . . . and talk of days when you could ride a pony from here to the high mountain camps without ever seeing a town or a fence . . ."

"Or a white man," Red Shirt added.

"Oh," Brannon teased, "Bridger, Meek, Smith, Walker . . . even old Bill Williams . . . they were always here, weren't they?"

"No. But the black robes, they truly have been here forever!" Red Shirt laughed. "The day is coming when there will only be room for corn-growers and milk cows. Perhaps The Brannon will work in a store and sell shoes to old ladies?"

"And Red Shirt will sit on a bench and sell his picture to little children for a penny," Brannon countered.

Both men sat on the boulders for a long time staring at the trail. Brannon watched a brown hawk swoop out of the clouds and dive down at the sparse sage. Then suddenly the hawk flapped its powerful wings and soared to the sky, clutching a mouse meal in its talon.

It was late in the afternoon when he finally spotted a cloud of dust up the trail. He reached over to kick Red Shirt awake and slammed his sore right toe into the Indian's leg.

Red Shirt glanced at the grimacing Brannon and then out at the approaching riders.

"Perhaps a woman gave you such an injury," he announced.

"I'm not going to talk about it," was the only reply.

SEVEN

"The odds are getting better," Brannon announced as he watched the dust clouds from the oncoming riders drift closer.

"There are eight," Red Shirt reported.

"Yeah . . . I thought there might have been ten of them."

"How many will stand and fight?" Red Shirt asked.

"Well, we might as well find out." Brannon laid his rifle across the boulder in front of him.

"They are too far. Your bullets will be buried in the dust," Red Shirt warned.

"Yep. That's just what they think. But if I get a good carry, I just might land this bullet somewhere in the vicinity of that lead horse . . . and just maybe it will spook and toss the rider."

Shouldering his own rifle and keeping his eyes on the riders, Red Shirt cautioned, "It will tell them where we stand."

"They know where we're at," Brannon mumbled. Aiming above the lead horse, trying to allow for the trajectory of the bullet, he squeezed the trigger. The report of the shot echoed off the boulders in the treeless mountains. At the same time a buckskin horse tumbled to the ground, slamming its rider to

134

the desert floor almost six hundred yards down the slope of the mountain.

"I think The Brannon just shot a horse!" Red Shirt spoke without expression or inflection.

"Oh . . . I don't think I hit it . . . did I? No, it just got frightened and . . . my word, I hit that buckskin!"

"One of the finest shots I have ever seen!" Red Shirt nodded without emotion. "However, The Brannon should not fire again and let them know how lucky he was the first time."

"You're right about that! Look, they're dismounting."

"And hiding? They must think we are closer than we are."

"Or they think we have a buffalo gun. Either way, they will slow down."

"And fan out. Some are spreading out to the left."

"And to the right." Brannon motioned.

"They are holding the horses back."

"That gives them a chance to ride away. Let them creep up to the base of the mountain. Then we'll fire a couple shots to sit them down. Maybe then we can palaver."

Brannon watched as the men below scurried from sage to sage, boulder to boulder. Clouds stacked up on the far side of the valley. The wind, blowing at his back, started to take on a slight chill.

"Which one is Trevor?" Red Shirt asked.

"I can't tell . . . it's been a long time since I've

seen him . . . maybe that one with the black hat. He seems to be giving directions."

"The one with gray hair?"

"Maybe . . . I can't tell, yet. Let's sit them down right there!"

Both Brannon and Red Shirt fired several shots at the line of men, who all quickly ducked behind rocks.

Cupping his hand to magnify his voice, Brannon shouted, "That's close enough, boys! I don't want anybody to get hurt!"

"You shot my horse, Brannon!" a deep voice boomed. "That's the second time you shot a horse out from under me!"

"Trevor? Is that you with the gray hair?"

"Ten years at the state prison ages a man."

"Not as much as a hangin'," Brannon shouted. "Trevor, you and the boys ride on back to New Mexico, and then I won't have to write a note to any of your mamas."

"We won't buy that, Brannon. Seems like some of the citizens of Arizona will pay big money for your carcass. But we don't need to shoot those Indians. Do they understand that their lives are in danger?"

Suddenly Red Shirt fired a shot in Trevor's direction that caused the gunman to dive behind a bigger rock.

"Does that tell you what the Ute thinks?" Brannon shouted.

"Brannon, you haven't got a chance!"

"That's what you told me up in Colorado,

Trevor. You boys go on home!" Brannon fired another shot at a man attempting to flank them on the right. The man scrambled back to the others.

Several shots ricocheted off the rock around Brannon.

"Now you boys are making me mad!" he shouted. "I was planning on givin' you a decent burial, but now I just might leave your bodies out here for the buzzards to pick clean!" He fired two more shots at a spot where several were gathered and then rolled over to a new location.

About half a dozen bullets hit his old hiding place.

"Now look, boys, this is a dead-end street for you. What did Trevor promise you anyway?"

"An eight-way split of $10,000!" one of them yelled. Red Shirt fired a bullet that sprayed granite all over the spokesman.

"You boys don't really think there's anybody in Arizona that will give you $10,000 to have me dead, do you? That's Trevor's lie to get you to do his grudge work. I'm not worth that much. Maybe he'll buy you supper and a drink at the saloon, but that's all you'll get. He's putting your life on the line for his revenge!"

Seeing one of the gunmen start to scoot back to the horses, Brannon raised his gun to fire at the man, and then held up.

"That's right . . . one of you is pulling out, and

he might be the only one who will dance with his Mary this Saturday night." He fired several random shots at the men that allowed the retreating man some freedom to reach his horse and ride off.

Red Shirt glanced at Brannon and held up seven fingers.

"You're a dead man, Brannon!" Trevor shouted. "I didn't think you were the type to endanger a woman and kid . . . even if they are Indian!"

"The boy handles that shotgun pretty well. I figure he'll gut-shoot at least two of ya . . . probably that old boy in the gray hat who keeps trying to sneak up on the left!"

Suddenly a blast from the shotgun rumbled from behind them and sent the man crawling on hands and knees back down the mountain. Brannon swung around and saw Littlefoot perched in the rocks above them.

"You're wasting bullets, Brannon!" Trevor shouted.

"Wasted? Nah . . . we've got enough ammunition to hold off Geronimo and the whole Chiricahua Apache nation. We've got plenty of water too. Do you boys have enough water? Maybe you'll get lucky and it'll rain. But don't you go dehydrating out there in the heat. If you need a drink, just walk right up here, and I'll give you one . . . yes sir, no one should die of thirst today."

"You're bluffin', Brannon!"

"You know me better than that, Trevor. Think about it, boys . . . there's a Ute chief up here. If he dies, do you think your life is going to be worth a cow chip? Yes sir, killing a sick woman and kid will make you about as popular as old Bob Ford!" Brannon fired two shots and began to sneak down the mountain toward the gunmen. Red Shirt moved downhill at the same time.

"I just want you, Brannon! I been waitin' ten long years! Send the others on their way!" Trevor shouted.

There was no response.

Several shots were fired at Brannon's previous position.

"Brannon!" Trevor yelled.

Meanwhile, Brannon crawled close enough to hear the conversation among those hiding in the rocks.

"Trevor, I don't hear him. Maybe we winged him."

"He's still up there!"

"Maybe he went up higher?"

"Yeah . . . you want to go and see?"

"I ain't goin' up there, no, sir!"

"Give me some cover, boys," another voice shouted. "I ain't 'fraid of no old man and one Injun!"

Bullets rang out toward Brannon and Red Shirt's former positions, and he could see a man break from the others and slowly work his way up the hill.

He's comin' right at me! Only he doesn't know I'm this close!

With Brannon on the left, Red Shirt on the right, and Littlefoot still perched up high on the mountain, they surrounded the trail up the mountain.

Brannon pulled out his Colt revolver and crouched low, waiting for the gunman to reach him. Coming to the cluster of boulders, the man dove for the rocks and unknowingly rolled himself to Brannon's feet.

Brannon jammed the hard steel barrel of a walnut-handled Peacemaker into the gunman's adam's apple so hard that the man dropped his weapon and gagged.

"You say a word, and you'll have a hole in your throat big enough to swallow biscuits whole!" Brannon growled.

"Swipe!" Trevor yelled. "Swipe, did you run into trouble?"

"Now you listen quick," Brannon commanded the trembling man. The only chance you got to live is to hike back down this hill, past the others, and down to your horse. You ride south, and I'll never think a thing about it. But if you head up this hill again, you'll be the first one I kill. Oh, we might not be able to shoot all of you, but you'll be dead long before the last bullet's fired. Do you understand me?"

The man shook his head so fast his hat tumbled to the dirt.

"Now you leave that pistol of yours lying in

the dirt. Pull off your gunbelt and your boots!"

"Swipe!" another of the men shouted. Then suddenly a dozen shots were fired up the mountainside.

Brannon shoved the weaponless and stocking-footed man out into the clearing.

"Hold your fire, boys!" Swipe hollered. "It's me! Hold your fire!"

Staying flat on the ground, Brannon peered around the boulders to watch the man's retreat. He slowly made his way toward the others, constantly stopping to pick sticks and rocks out of his socks.

"What happened, Swipe?"

"Where's your boots?"

"Where's your gun?"

"Did he take your gun?"

"This ain't my fight no more, Trevor!" Swipe shouted. Brannon saw the man light-foot his way past the other's hiding place and head to the horses.

Brannon noticed that the man who had stayed with the horses mounted up and rode off with Swipe.

Five. It's down to five.

Another of the men broke toward the milling horses, but this time Brannon's shots from the Winchester caused him to dive back for protection.

Don't you all leave at once. There's a little business to take care of —

"He's over in those rocks, boys. We've got him

141

pinned down now!" Trevor shouted.

Having revealed how close he was, Brannon now sensed his danger. He was too low to follow their lateral movement. He could hear the scuffle of boots and knew they were circling his position.

All right, Red Shirt. Now would be an excellent time to move them back.

He searched off to the right to see signs of the Ute chief.

Maybe even a blast of that old shotgun will slow them down.

He glanced up at Littlefoot's position, but didn't see anything.

"Hey! He's got the horses!" one of the men shouted.

"Shoot that kid!"

Brannon chanced a look out from behind the rocks in time to see Littlefoot riding a bay horse, leading the other three horses down the hill. Rifle fire from straight left of the gunmen caused them to dive to new places of safety and revealed their positions to Brannon.

Littlefoot! Lord, protect him. He's as crazy as his . . . kind of like . . . me, isn't he?

"You boys know you're in big trouble now. If you want to ride out of here . . . well, I'll try to talk that Indian kid out of shootin' ya. 'Course he's really wantin' to scalp a couple of ya, so you bald-headed men probably have the best chance. Any of you bald?"

"Give me my horse, Brannon, and I'll ride!" one of the men shouted.

"Which is your horse?"

"The gray gelding!"

Brannon wasn't sure Littlefoot was within hearing distance, but he glanced out to see the gray horse cut out of the band and trotting out into the desert.

"Your horse is heading for the desert. If you hurry, you can catch him!" Brannon shouted.

The man sprinted for the valley floor and dove behind some sage before anyone could stop him. Finally, he ran across the desert with his horse trotting ahead of him.

"You boys are surrounded now . . . you plan on giving up, or do we have to start tossing in the lead?"

A dozen shots clipped granite near his head, one piece striking his left eye, causing him to dive flat on the ground and grab his eye with his left hand. He worked the rock sliver out of his eyelid, but noticed his vision in that eye was blurred.

"You boys want out of this alive?" he shouted.

"We got you out-gunned, Brannon!" Trevor shouted.

"The lady's a good shot, too. A minute ago you had eight men, and I'm getting tired of talk. Hogtie Trevor and toss him into this clearing, and I'll let you all ride out of here . . . that's my last offer. I'm not talking anymore!" Brannon thundered. He shoved more shells into the breech of his Winchester and crawled out from behind the rocks to the protection of a clump of sagebrush. He still couldn't focus with his left eye.

He heard several shots among the gunmen, and then a body was rolled out from behind the boulders.

"He ain't dead, Brannon, but he'll have a headache when he wakes up. You tie him yourself. Now are you goin' to keep your word?"

"You boys stand with your backs to me!" he shouted.

"Don't let them Indians shoot us!"

"I said stand up with your backs to me!" Brannon hollered.

Slowly, three men stood, facing downhill.

"Turn out the horses, Littlefoot!" he yelled.

Brannon heard a whoop and a holler, and the remaining horses scurried down toward the open desert with the gunmen hustling after them.

Brannon, Littlefoot, and Red Shirt all reached Trevor at the same time.

"Is he dead?" Red Shirt asked.

Brannon rolled his body over.

"Nope. Not even shot."

"What about the shooting?" Littlefoot quizzed. "I heard three shots."

"Just a friendly argument, I suppose. Run up there and get me a rope." He motioned to Red Shirt. "Littlefoot, you go check on your mother. She's apt to be worried sick."

"What's wrong with your eye? It's bleeding!" Littlefoot inquired.

"Oh . . . it's nothin' . . . some rock chips."

"The Brannon is very tough," Red Shirt explained. He bumped his toe on a pebble, and a grain of sand has blown into his eye. It is certainly the sign of old age."

The Indian turned to retrieve the rope, and Brannon couldn't tell if Red Shirt was smiling or not.

After tying Trevor's hands and feet, Brannon and Red Shirt trudged back up the hill toward their camp.

"You going to leave him down there?" Red Shirt asked.

"At least until he wakes up."

"How will you know when he's awake?"

"I didn't gag him . . . we'll know."

Entering the camp, he walked over to Elizabeth and Littlefoot.

"You've got a brave warrior there." He nodded at Littlefoot.

"Yes," she whispered. "I know."

"Fighting alongside of The Brannon makes many brave," Red Shirt added.

"I don't know what that has to do with — "

"Like the great chiefs of old, The Brannon acts like he is confident of winning every battle. Soon those around him begin to believe it too. And when he talks the enemy into believing it, the battle is over."

"Well, not many men will risk death on another man's rancor." Brannon shrugged.

"What will you do with the man Trevor?" Littlefoot asked.

"I believe he should just leave him tied out in the desert," Red Shirt proposed.

"I guess I'll haul him into Medicine Hat and turn him over to the authorities. I think attempted murder is still a crime, and he must have broke out of prison."

"When will we leave?" Elizabeth asked.

"It's just a long day's journey, so we can haul out of here at daybreak tomorrow. We should hit the main road about evening, and maybe I'll catch you a wagon ride to town."

"I would like to go now," she offered.

"What? Now? It's almost dark, and —"

"I feel strong. I do not believe I will have many strong days left. I want to see the shade of the fruit trees at your ranch . . . and the cattle on the mountain behind it."

"How do you know . . ."

"Littlefoot has told me it is the most beautiful ranch in the world." She tried to smile.

"In the springtime you should see the green grass in the valley . . . and the flowers along Sunrise Creek . . . red, orange, purple, and yellows . . . oh, wait until you see the spring," he encouraged her.

"I will be grateful to see it anytime. Could we leave now? This mountain does not make me happy. What has happened to your eye? It looks red."

"He doesn't want to talk about that either," Littlefoot teased.

Within minutes they were all packed and mounted.

"Brannon, I'll kill you!" a distant shout echoed up the mountain.

"Trevor just woke up from his rifle-barrel nap!" Brannon announced.

"Red Shirt, if you lasso that hombre and run him up here, we're ready to roll out."

The impassive Ute turned in the saddle and almost smiled.

"The enemy is on a leash like a dog. I believe it will be a boring journey."

"Well, that's probably right. We should be — "

"So I believe it is time for Red Shirt to return home to the fires of his own family."

Brannon sighed and pushed his hat back on his head and nodded.

"Brannon, I know you're up there! I'll kill you! You're a dead man, Brannon!"

"Your dog is barking," Red Shirt declared.

"You take care of yourself. And for heaven's sake, don't ever change. This whole West is changing . . . everyone but you and me," Brannon concluded.

"I will expect a visit from The Brannon. You have promised to tell me about your Jesus. I think I like this Jesus. He is better than the Jesus that the others try to tell me about."

"I'll meet you at the peaches . . . next summer," Brannon promised.

"Will you help the women pick the fruit?" Red Shirt asked.

"I will work as hard as Red Shirt," Brannon teased.

Suddenly Red Shirt smiled from ear to ear. "Then The Brannon will not work at all! You can bring your son as well." He nodded at Littlefoot.

"Oh . . . he's not . . ." Brannon paused and noticed Elizabeth's stare.

"Yes, of course I'll bring Littlefoot."

"Good." Red Shirt nodded. The smile had melted to noncommitment. "I have a daughter about his age." Red Shirt flung a salute, kicked his horse, and galloped down the mountain into the desert.

"Don't let the Indian kill me, Brannon!" Trevor shouted from down the mountain.

Elizabeth watched Red Shirt depart. "He is a good man."

"Will we really go to see him in the peaches?" Littlefoot asked.

"Yep."

"But the trip will be too difficult for mother," Littlefoot cautioned.

Brannon glanced down at Elizabeth. He thought he could see tears welling up in the corners of her eyes.

"By next summer your mother is going to be in perfect health," Brannon assured him. "Now you go down there and cut his foot rope and then lead him up here. We'll let him march in front of Dos Vientos."

Most of the trip that evening was down the gradual slope and across the flat desert floor. They plodded along, Elizabeth on the travois, Brannon riding the big black horse, Trevor grumbling and walking with arms bound and tethered in front, and Littlefoot prancing on the pinto from one side of the trail to the other, always circling back to check on his mother. They stopped often to rest the horses.

Elizabeth was awake all night. She didn't cough until daylight.

They crossed the road that ran south to Medicine Hat about noon the next day. Spotting no one on the road, Brannon turned the others toward town. Within a few minutes he heard hooves pound the desert floor. There was a squeak of wheels, a rattle of boards, and a shout from the driver as a stagecoach lunged over the rise behind them. He ushered Littlefoot to the side of the road.

"I'll catch your mother a ride on the stage," he shouted. He waved a salute to the driver as the stagecoach pulled up. The man riding next to the driver threw his gun to his shoulder and pointed it at Brannon as they roared past. A little boy in the stage waved to them but had his arm jerked back inside.

The dust was so thick that Brannon couldn't see Trevor who remained tight at the end of the rope. Finally, it cleared a little, and Brannon, as well as Elizabeth, began to cough.

"They were probably running on a tight schedule. We'll catch another ride," he reassured her.

About a half hour later a man on a farm wagon rumbled down the road. This time Brannon purposely stayed in the roadway and waved for the man to stop. At the last minute the wagon swerved out into the desert but didn't slow.

"You Indians get off the road!" the man yelled as he sped on toward town.

Brannon led the others off the road and out into the clear air. He glanced around at Littlefoot, Elizabeth on the travois, Trevor covered from head to toe in road dust, and himself in beaded deerskin shirt and moccasins.

Lord, forgive them. They aren't going to stop for us Indians, are they?

Riding out so he could be upwind and parallel to the road, they continued the journey. He didn't bother trying anymore to flag a ride, nor did he wave at those on the road.

Step after step.

Hill after hill.

Mile after mile.

Finally, in the distance he could see trees, buildings . . . and people scurrying about. A trail of cottonwoods wound into town from the north and out of town to the south. The buildings sprang out of the ground like a manicured garden in an otherwise barren field.

They worked their way to the city limits of Medicine Hat. The straight streets, painted buildings, and fenced yards of the town marked a sharp contrast to the rugged desert landscape that surrounded it. Brannon felt out of place and uncomfortable as they trudged down the main street.

Folks along the way either ignored them completely or stopped to stare at the strange parade. Brannon's first stop was the city marshal's office.

The sign on the door read "Albert S. Young, Marshal & Mayor." As Littlefoot helped Elizabeth out of the travois, Brannon marched Trevor into the marshal's office. A man looked up from trying to start a fire in the pot-bellied stove. His face was familiar.

"Reyn . . . Reynolds?"

The balding man in the vested suit squinted his eyes. "We don't handle no Injun matters. You'll have to take that up with the agent on the . . . what? . . . don't tell me." The man broke into a wide grin. "Stuart Brannon? Heavens, you do look tuckered out . . . and a tad older, I might add."

"Reynolds, are you the marshal in Medicine Hat?"

"No, sir, Mr. Brannon, just one of the deputies. Say, I read about how you put down that rebellion in South America. Yes, sir, and you did it almost single-handed — just you and the local girl Juanita. That was quite something!"

"I presume you've been reading Hawthorne Miller again?"

"Yep. I never missed a one of 'em. I got all twenty-six volumes, I do." Then he glanced over at the dust-covered Trevor. "Who's he?"

"Reynolds, I want you to lock Trevor up for me, and I'll stop by later and explain to the marshal. He's been following me across the desert for a week trying to bushwhack me and some others. So hold him for attempted murder, but check your papers. I figure he escaped from prison over in New Mexico. He was serving a long term for killing the sheriff of Tres Casas."

"Yes, sir, Mr. Brannon. I'll lock him up. Soon as I find the keys, that is. I know they're here in the desk . . . we don't have many customers . . . I mean, this is the first time I've had to lock anyone up. Here they are!" He turned and led Trevor to a cell.

"How long you been a deputy?" Brannon asked.

"Oh, about three years now," Read Reynolds replied.

"Well, you can untie him before you lock him up." Brannon motioned.

"Yes, sir, I'll do that!"

"Tell the marshal we'll be staying at the hotel. Say, what's the best hotel in town?"

"The Deseret," Reynolds offered. But I'd change shirts if I was you."

"Why's that?" Brannon asked.

" 'Cause they might not let you in being that dirty, and they for sure wouldn't let no one in that looked like an Injun."

Brannon stared at the nervous man.

"They'll let me in," he asserted.

They didn't.

Not the Deseret.

Not the Illinois Garden.

Not the Top Hat.

An hour later he finally secured two rooms at Mrs. Hinson's Boarding House only because Elizabeth collapsed on the porch, and Mrs. Hinson felt obliged to take her in.

"It's only until she gets to feeling better," she insisted. "Does she speak English? Does she sleep in a bed? I hear they prefer to sleep on the floor. I'll serve your meals in your rooms. No reason to disturb the other boarders. Your rooms are near the back door. I'm sure you'll find it convenient to use the back door. My, she is ill. She will be all right, won't she? I mean I wouldn't want . . . oh, it will be two dollars for the rooms. I need to have the money in advance. It's my policy. I suppose you'll be leaving tomorrow?"

Brannon paid the woman and brought Elizabeth and Littlefoot into the big room. He tossed his gear on a little screen porch at the back next to a cot.

"Littlefoot, you stay here with your mother.

I'm going to find a doctor, check with the marshal, and buy us a wagon. I don't think we want to stay in this town long."

"I do not want to stay in it at all!" Littlefoot announced.

Brannon gazed down at Elizabeth who had already fallen asleep on top of the feather-soft bed.

"Well, neither do I . . . but your mother deserves some rest. You might take that basin and wash the trail dust off the two of you. The lady said she'd bring supper to us, but I'll be back by then."

"Perhaps we can leave by morning," Littlefoot suggested.

Brannon nodded and left the house by the back door. He checked the horses into a livery that smelled like wet hay and fresh manure, and then he hiked up the stairs of a neat two-story building just down the block.

"What do you want?" a gruff voice greeted him as he entered.

Brannon looked up to see a large woman wearing a long green dress. It was buttoned so tight at the neck that it seemed to be the only thing that kept her from exploding.

"Eh . . . I'd like to speak to the doctor."

"Are you Indian?"

"No . . . but what difference does that make?"

"Indians are suppose to use reservation doctors," she insisted. "Doctor's busy anyway."

Brannon peeked behind a white cloth divider

154

and noticed a man sleeping on a cot.

"Wake him up!" Brannon demanded.

"I will do no such thing! Now if you don't leave I'll — "

Brannon pulled his Colt from the holster and shoved his hat back with the barrel. Using it as a pointer, he continued, "there's a woman down at the boarding house that's dyin', and I'm a cash-paying customer. Now wake up that doctor and tell him Stuart Brannon needs some medical assistance!"

"Brannon? The . . . the . . . *the* Stuart Brannon, the gunman from Arizona? The one in the history books?"

"I reckon that's the one." He nodded.

"But . . . I thought . . . I thought you died years ago. I — "

"Wake up the doctor, please."

Within a few minutes Dr. Andrew P. Smith, Jr., was scurrying toward Mrs. Hinson's Boarding House. Brannon noticed that the sky was overcast and the clouds hung low.

His next stop was a general store where the clerk ignored him until he heard the jingle of Brannon's gold coins. He left the store wearing new boots and a new shirt, carrying his moccasins and deerskin shirt in a bundle under his left arm.

Spying a sign in a window advertising a wagon for sale, he entered the building and spent twenty minutes concluding a deal for a farm wagon and two pulling horses. Then he crossed the street and pushed open the door at the marshal's office.

"Reynolds, did the — " Brannon did not see Read Reynolds at the stove nor Trevor behind bars. Instantly he reached for his revolver. Cold, hard steel pressed against the back of his neck.

"Don't touch that weapon, Mister!" a voice commanded.

Slowly, Brannon turned around to see a short, thin man wearing a badge.

"You the marshal?"

"Yep. Now loosen that belt and let the gun drop to the floor."

Brannon complied. "Marshal, look, I'm the one pressing charges against Trevor. What happened to him? Did he bust out?"

"Nope," the marshal continued. "Now you just back right on over to that cell."

"What? You got this wrong! Trevor's been trying to kill me for a week, and I brought him — "

"That ain't the story I heard. He claims you shot his horse, stole his saddle, and kidnapped him," the marshal reported.

"He said what?"

"You heard me!"

"And you believed him?"

"Yep. There was a man who passed through here yesterday said the same thing. Said he took a nasty wound from a squawman out in the desert. I figure that was you!"

"He was one of Trevor's hired guns! Of course I wasn't going to let him shoot a lady!" Brannon watched in disbelief as the marshal locked him behind the bars of the cell.

"Look," Brannon contended, "I've got witnesses. Go down there to the boarding house and ask Littlefoot and Elizabeth. They'll tell you —"

"We don't need any Indian testimony. We've got all the evidence we need. You're being held for attempted murder, theft, horse-killin', and kidnappin'."

"You're making a big mistake," Brannon roared. "Let me talk to someone . . . the mayor! Where's the mayor?"

"I am the mayor."

"The judge? You have a judge in this town?"

"Yep. But father's out hunting quail today. You'll have to wait until tomorrow."

"You got a telegraph in this town?"

"Of course we do."

"Then I want to wire the governor of Arizona in Tucson, and tell him that Stuart Brannon is being held on false charges in Medicine Hat, Utah."

"Are you claimin' to be Stuart Brannon?"

"I AM Stuart Brannon!"

"Yeah, and I'm Billy the Kid."

EIGHT

"What other lies did Trevor tell you?"

"Lies? Look, mister, you're hardly in a position to call the kettle black. What he told me was that you were a drifter he met in a prison in New Mexico. You were mad at him about some mutual girlfriend in Santa Fe . . . and you tried to kill him out in the desert, but were afraid to do it in front of the Indian woman and her kid."

"Met him in jail! I sent him to jail for killing a sheriff in Tres Casas," Brannon shouted. "He was supposed to be hung, but got off with life in prison. He's an escaped convict — that's what he is!"

"I can assure you the volume of your voice will not prove your innocence, so you might as well calm down," the marshal persisted. "Now, as for Trevor's prison term, he fully admitted his past and informed me of the pardon issued by the governor of the territory."

"What? A pardon? That can't be. He's a killer!"

"A reformed killer. He says he has a full pardon."

"Did you actually see the pardon?"

"No, he said it was on the horse you shot out from under him."

"Telegraph New Mexico and confirm that," Brannon commanded.

"I see no need for that."

"Are you going to telegraph the governor of Arizona for me?"

"There is no need for that either."

Brannon stormed back and forth in the small cell. "I just don't have time to play this little game! There's a sick woman down at the boarding house that's counting on my taking care of her. Set a bail figure, and I'll post a bond. Then I'll stay in town until we can get this solved."

"You shot one man and are trying to kill another. I'm afraid you're too desperate a character to allow on the streets of Medicine Hat, Mr. . . . what is your name?"

"Brannon! I'm Stuart Brannon!"

The marshal pulled off his hat and waved it at the jail cell. "I've had about enough of this Brannon stuff. Last week we had a guy through here who claimed to be Col. Custer. The week before that we had the Emperor of Mexico. And three weeks ago, there was a tall blonde cowhand who had most of the town convinced he was none other than the Arizona legend — Stuart Brannon. So how about coming up with something original because I'm getting tired of all you Stuart Brannons!"

"Where's Reynolds? Get Read Reynolds. He can identify me!"

"Mr. Reynolds seems to be busy. I can't find

him anywhere," the marshal reported.

"He what? . . . Trevor! Did Reynolds disappear about the time you let Trevor out?"

"Well, I can't say . . . I suppose . . . anyway, you've got to stay in jail until the judge hears the case. I suppose that will be the day after tomorrow."

Brannon leaned against the iron bars and waved his hands at the marshal. "Listen, there's a dying woman in the boarding house! I don't intend to sit here in this cell for two days on some trumped-up charge while she dies; do you understand?"

"Oh, yeah, I understand. You are threatening an elected official. That, too, is a crime — to be added to your charges!"

"Threatening?" Brannon roared. "That wasn't threatening! If I'd told you that I'm going to bust out of here, hogtie you, and toss you over the rim of the Grand Canyon, that would be threatening! Or if I'd shouted that I'll hang you by your heels from a tall tree and peel your hide off in one-inch strips, that would be threatening!"

"Mister," the marshal stopped him, "that's all the talk I want to hear from you! I'll put a man outside this front door, but he doesn't have to sit in here and listen to your ranting!"

Brannon turned and smashed his black hat against the back wall of the cell. Then he whipped around toward the exiting sheriff.

"Wait! Look . . . it's extremely important that

I get word to the woman and her son at the boarding house. Could you ask the boy to come see me so I can explain the situation . . . for God's sake, tell the boy where I am."

"Don't go cursing at me," the marshal roared.

"I can assure you, Marshal, I did not use God's name in disrespect. I have survived forty years in this country only by His grace and mercy. And I will, with His help, survive this present situation as well!"

The marshal stared at Brannon and then glanced down at the floor. "I'll see that someone tells the boy." He turned and left the office.

Brannon walked to the back of the cell and retrieved his hat. Then he collapsed on the hard wooden bunk that served as the cell's only furniture. The room smelled dusty and stuffy. When he rubbed his face, he could feel the stubble of a week's beard and the road dirt of days on the desert. His eye no longer blurred but still felt raw, and the pain in his toe pulsed from barely noticeable to severe.

Lord, this is a mess. All I want is to take Elizabeth and Littlefoot back to the ranch. I don't know how in the world I ended up in here. I don't want to break any laws, but I've got to get back to the boarding house. I couldn't live with myself if she died while I was in jail. So either help me figure this thing out, or send an angel to open the cell because I've —

The front door of the office banged open, and Brannon jumped to his feet.

"Reynolds! What in the world happened to you?" Brannon called.

Reynolds staggered into the room, blood trickling down beside his left eye. Holding his sides and coughing, he threw himself down in the marshal's chair and tried to catch his breath.

"Did you get run over by a wagon? You need a doctor. There's a doctor down at the Hinson's. Send that deputy out front for the doctor."

"Cain't."

"What?"

"I done sent him to find Marshal Young." Gasping for air, Reynolds continued, "I think he broke my ribs!"

"Who? Who beat you up like that?"

"Some bushwhacker hidin' in the alley beside the Illinois Garden Hotel, that's who."

"Was it Trevor?"

Reynolds just stared at him.

"Was it the man I brought in? Did you know the marshal turned him loose?"

"Yeah, I heard the marshal was after you. But it don't make no sense . . . no, sir, how he could believe — "

"Read, was it Trevor who bushwhacked you?" Brannon pressured.

Reynolds, still clutching his sides, took a deep breath and looked around the room.

"Mr. Brannon, you know I ain't a brave man. He said that if I identified you, he would kill me! I got a wife and two little babies now. I

162

need this job. I mean, it ain't much to a man like you, but it's all I got. I'm scared. I'm real scared. Now if you was out, if you was on the street to face that man down, well, I might have a little more courage, but I'm mighty scared and hurtin'."

"Read, haul yourself down to the Hinson's house right now. You got to get patched up. Listen to me. I'm going to figure a way out of this and settle up with Trevor. You go take care of the wife and babies."

"Yes, sir, Mr. Brannon. Yes, sir . . . I will."

"If you see an Indian boy down there, tell him to come see me. I need to talk to him."

"Thanks, Mr. Brannon. I surely do wish I was brave enough to face him down by myself."

"Go on, Read . . . get yourself fixed up and go home and hug those babies."

"Yes, sir, yes, sir . . . I'll go home, but I don't figure to hug nothin' for a while!" Reynolds limped to the door. "Mr. Brannon, I been thinkin' maybe it's time to move. You got any work down Arizona way?"

"Read, you come down to Prescott. I've got friends that can give you a job there."

"Thanks, Mr. Brannon . . . thanks."

Reynolds hadn't been gone for two minutes before Marshal Young and another man burst through the door.

"Where's Reynolds? Did he go off and leave you unguarded? That's the last —"

"Reynolds is seriously injured. He got bush-

163

whacked beside the hotel, and I sent him to a doctor."

"You sent him to a doctor? A driftin' cowhand in jail tells my deputies what to do?"

"The man is hurt bad, Marshal. Look . . . I'm still here in the cell, so there's no harm done."

"Groten, you stay here! I'll try to find Reynolds," the marshal ordered as he shoved his way back out into the street.

While the front door was still swinging, Littlefoot rushed in. The deputy named Groten whipped around and yanked awkwardly at his revolver that was caught in his holster.

"Wait!" Brannon called. "It's just a kid. He came to see me."

"We don't allow no Injuns in Medicine Hat!" the man reported.

"You telling me you're afraid of this boy?" Brannon chided.

"No, it ain't that . . ."

"Good, then I'm sure you won't mind him talking to me. Littlefoot, how's your mother?"

"She's sleeping. The doctor gave her some purple drink. It made her sleepy. What is The Brannon doing in the cage?"

"You see, Deputy, what did he call me?"

"I don't believe no Injuns!"

"Littlefoot, there's been a big mistake here. They let Trevor out and locked me up."

"But he was trying to kill us!"

"Yeah, well, I'm having a hard time convincing them of that. Now listen to me. You go straight back to your mother and don't leave her side. You get out that shotgun, and if Trevor comes after you, you'll have to protect your mother. Do you understand what I'm saying?"

"Yes, sir."

"I'm going to get this thing straightened out in a little while. I'll probably be there by suppertime. Now go on, and stay off the streets."

Littlefoot raced out of the office.

"Say," the deputy asked, "you ain't the real Stuart Brannon, is ya?"

"That's what I've been trying to tell everyone since I came to town — a destination that I'm now strongly regretting!"

"Well . . . ain't that nice. Medicine Hat, Utah — the town that lassoed the Arizona legend. That might put us on the map. Providin' of course that you are the real Brannon." The deputy shook his head and moseyed back outside.

The only light in the marshal's office streamed through the small four-pane window in the front of the building. With the door closed, the office was dark and musty. Brannon sat down, pulled off his new boot, and rubbed his sore foot. Then he gingerly replaced the boot and began to pace back and forth in the eight-by-eight-foot cell. The only sound he could hear was the clomp of his own boot heels and the jingle of his spurs.

Brannon had stomped the jail cell for almost an hour before the marshal returned. The light-complected man ambled into the office, lifted off his round hat, dusted the brim, and hung it carefully on the first peg next to the door. Then he strolled over to his desk and sat down without looking toward Brannon.

"Well, how's Reynolds? Is he all right?" Brannon blurted out.

"The deputy took a severe beating."

"I know that. Did he tell you who did it?"

"Mr. Reynolds was unable to identify his assailant. Now how many men rode into town with you? Rumor has it you might have an accomplice in town."

"With me? Are you claiming that someone I know was responsible for the attack on Reynolds?"

"All I know is that there seems to be little other motive."

"What about Trevor? Maybe he did it."

"Why on earth for?"

"Just maybe I am Stuart Brannon. Just maybe Reynolds could have identified me. Just maybe Trevor did try to kill me in the desert. Just maybe he escaped from a New Mexico prison. Did that ever cross your narrow mind?" Brannon hollered.

"Mister, I've had all the rampages I'm going to take from you. If you continue to behave in such a manner, I'll have you bound and gagged. Do you understand?"

Brannon stood in silence for a moment. Then he spoke in a low voice. "Yeah . . . you're right. I offer my apologies for the tone and volume of my voice. I have some difficulty controlling my anger when I'm illegally imprisoned and when a woman who's counting on me lays dying in a boarding house down the street."

The marshal pulled a book out of his desk. "I asked Reynolds if he could identify you as Stuart Brannon, and he said it was difficult because he hadn't seen Brannon in years. But I do have a way you can identify yourself."

"Oh?"

"Well, Reynolds left one of his Brannon of the Wild West novels here. Now I suppose if you could tell me some of the events in this story, I'd have a better chance of believin' you."

"Marshal, you aren't serious. Those things were written in New York City by Hawthorne Miller. It's all fiction! He makes the stories up."

"Sounds like you're tryin' to weasel out of this. I'm sure Miller takes some literary license, but surely you could remember the main events of your own life. Okay, here's the first question. What was the name of the horse that you bought while in Argentina?"

"Argentina? I've never been to — "

"Seems like you would remember Chico the horse. After all, he saved your life up in that mountain pass."

"He did what?"

"How much money did you recover from the

bank robbers down in Bolivia?"

"Look, I was never — "

"100,000 U.S. dollars. How could you forget such an easy number?" The marshal continued to flip through the book. "And the little boy that you rescued from the Bengal tiger — what was his name?"

"Tigers? They don't have tigers in South America!"

"Obviously you forgot about the circus train wreck. The boy's name was Edwardo. And the lovely Spanish lady who captured your affections — what was her name?"

"Eh . . . ," Brannon stammered, "Juanita?"

"Hardly. It was Carmelita."

"Carmelita?"

"You know less about Stuart Brannon than I do. Now I want a straight answer. Who are you?"

"I've explained that until I'm sick of it. Look, can you do this for me? Just let me out of here so I can go down and talk to the sick woman. You can put me in shackles, surround me with armed guards, and shoot me if I try to escape, but let me talk to the lady."

"The rules won't allow me to let you out of that cell until the judge orders it. You're just going to have to wait until then."

"Have you wired the governor of Arizona?"

"Mister, we aren't payin' for any telegram. Besides, it don't matter who you are. Crime is crime. Now I've got more important things to do. I've got to find which drunken cowboy bush-whacked my deputy."

"I'd start by checking out Trevor," Brannon suggested.

"Your vengeance toward Trevor is unrelenting. That's why you'll remain behind bars. I'll not have you shooting that man in the back on the streets of Medicine Hat!" The marshal pulled his hat back on and marched out the door.

Brannon could see a deputy stationed out on the wooden sidewalk in front. After standing and staring out the front window at the street for several minutes, he turned and lay down on his back on the wooden bunk. Folding his hands under his head for a pillow, he tried to close his eyes. The wood was extremely hard, and his leg and his shoulder started to ache at the same time. He tried to scrunch to a better position.

He couldn't find one.

Lord, it's all like a bad dream. I just want to wake up and get on with taking care of Eliza-beth. I don't want to fight this marshal or the town or even Trevor. I just want to get on down the road toward the ranch. It sure would be good to get some rest. But how can a man sleep when someone needs him? I don't like feeling so helpless. So I guess it's up to You now. I don't think the Stuart Brannon of fact . . . or fiction can figure this thing out.

For another five minutes Brannon tried to

think of an explanation that would free him from jail.

Finding no solution, he spent the next five minutes considering possible ways to escape.

That, too, was futile.

Then something unexpected happened.

He fell asleep.

Having not slept in over thirty-six hours, it was a deep, heavy, dreamless slumber of a body that was exhausted. In his sleep, he no longer worried about Elizabeth . . . nor Little-foot . . . nor Trevor. It was a difficult kind of sleep to wake up from, and when he finally felt someone poking him in the side, he sat up in bed and fumbled to pull his missing Peace-maker out of a nonexistent holster.

"Mr. Brannon!" a shallow voice whispered. "Mr. Brannon, wake up!"

"Where am I?" he mumbled, groping for his hat.

"You're still in jail, Mr. Brannon . . . it's me, Read Reynolds."

"Jail? Read? Medicine Hat. Oh . . . Read, how are you feeling?"

"Like I been run over by a herd of buffalo . . . but the doc fixed me up some."

"What are you doing in my cell? You didn't get arrested too?"

"Nope. I'm in here 'cause you didn't wake up when I hollered to you."

"Is it after dark?"

"Yep."

Brannon stood to his feet. "What's wrong?"

"Well, I was walking over to take my turn on guard, and I notices a lamp burnin' in the back room at Hinson's Boarding House. I go over there to see how your friends is doin' and find the boy in tears. He says there's a rattle in his mama's breathing, and she don't talk to him no more. He's feared she's dying, and he don't know what to do. He begs me to come tell you . . . so here I am."

"Read, I've got to go see them. You've got to let me out."

"If I'm caught, you know I'll lose my job."

"I know, I know. Listen, Read, you've got to do what's best for you and your family. I told you that earlier. But those two are about as close as I have to family, and . . . well, I've got to do my best by them as well. Now if you're willing, you can walk me down there at gunpoint, guard me all night, and march me back here before your shift is over."

"Yeah, I been considering that."

"On the other hand, if you can't do that . . ." Brannon feigned lying back down, but as he did, he yanked Read's gun from the holster. "Well," he continued, "we can march down there with me holding the gun. Which way would you prefer, Read?"

"Actually, Mr. Brannon, it's a toss-up. I get fired either way. But, if you don't mind, I'd rather hold the gun. At least it will make it look like I'm still in charge."

"You got it, Read." Brannon handed the revolver, grip-first, back to Reynolds.

Brannon stepped lightly across the wood floor and out into the night. The blast of cool fresh air smelled of rain.

"Has it rained?" Brannon whispered.

"Only a sprinkle," Read replied. "But it can cut loose at any minute. How about us staying off the sidewalks? Ain't no use wakin' up the neighborhood with boot heels crashing along."

After a couple of blocks of fresh air, Brannon felt wide awake. Kerosene lanterns flickered from the houses and shops of Medicine Hat. Brannon heard no shouts or curses or shots fired from drunken cowboys or miners.

I could just hogtie Reynolds, grab Elizabeth and Littlefoot, and ride south. They won't follow me across the border, and then maybe . . . Lord, You know I can't do that. But I want to do that. I want to do that real bad. You've got to help me do the right thing now.

Skirting around several buildings, they ducked through a two-story construction project that was only half-completed. Then they turned toward the boarding house. Brannon kicked on the back step with his left foot to bounce the mud off his boot. Then he kicked his right foot and felt a horrible pain shoot up his foot and leg. Biting his lip to keep from crying out, he felt his teeth puncture his lower lip. Blood started to trickle down his chin. He brushed his new shirt across his mouth, pulled open the screen door on the back porch, and softly walked into the house. Reynolds, gun in hand, followed one step behind.

The room was dimly lit by a kerosene lantern that needed its wick trimmed. In the flickering shadows Brannon could see Elizabeth in the bed, covers pulled around her body, and only a pallid, ashen face showing. Half-sitting, half-lying beside her, with his face on the tear-drenched pillow, was Littlefoot. Both seemed to be asleep.

Brannon reached down and touched the boy's shoulder, and Littlefoot sat erect and rubbed his eyes. Then, without a word spoken, he threw his arms around Brannon's neck and sobbed.

Brannon sat on the edge of the bed and hugged the boy. One of his arms held Littlefoot tight, and the other cradled his head. He began to rock the boy back and forth. Glancing over at Reynolds, he noticed that the deputy had reholstered his revolver and was brushing back tears from his own eyes.

The next few minutes seemed like hours. No one said a word. Finally, Littlefoot wiped his face on a sheet and glanced back at his mother.

"She has not spoken to me all night. She is dying. I don't want her to die! I don't want her to . . . die without saying good-bye."

When he heard Littlefoot's plea, Brannon couldn't hold back any longer. Tears flooded out of his eyes. Scenes of his wife's death filled his mind. Soon he began to hear his own sobs and realized that it was Littlefoot who was now trying to comfort him.

Finally, Brannon stood to his feet and walked over to a wash basin on the dresser. Soaking a clean towel, he washed his face and then returned to the bed and sat on the opposite side from Littlefoot. He stroked the matted hair back from Elizabeth's face and slipped his fingers along her neck to feel a faint pulse.

"Read, can you go roust out Doctor Smith?"

"Mr. Brannon . . . you know I cain't go off and leave a prisoner. What if you was to . . ."

"Reynolds," Brannon spoke with authority, "if there is anything in the world that you can count on, it's that I'll be right here when you get back. You're a family man. You know there is no way I'm going to leave this room with this woman hurting like this."

"Oh . . . I understand. I guess . . . shoot, Mr. Brannon, I'll go try and get the doc to come over. It's just that he don't much like doctoring in the middle of the night, especially when the patient's an . . . I mean, an . . ."

"Read, I know exactly what you mean. Tell the doctor I'll pay him double, and tell him how serious this is. I'll be right here. You can count on that."

"Well, they kin only fire me once!" Reynolds sighed. He quietly slipped out the back door and was gone.

With Littlefoot at his side, Brannon propped

up Elizabeth so she could breathe easier and began to wipe her forehead with the damp towel.

"Do you remember when your mother was young and pretty?" Brannon asked the boy.

"My mother has always been old," he reported.

"No, that's not true. Now when I first met her . . . well, she had plenty of cuts and bruises, and she was nine months pregnant with you, but she was a handsome girl. By spring she had her health back, and she was one of the two or three prettiest women I've ever met."

Brannon paused, and they both stared at the frail shell of a woman who lay on the bed.

"Tell me more about Mother," Littlefoot urged.

"Well, I didn't know her very long. She left that spring with her brother . . . I guess that was your uncle."

"Yes, I know the story. My uncle died at the battle of the Big Hole. I have no family but my mother."

"Son, your mother deserves a whole lot more than she got in this life, so I figure the Lord will make up for it all when she reaches Heaven."

"What is Heaven like?" Littlefoot asked.

"I've never been there, mind you, but I hear it's a wonderful place with golden streets, jeweled buildings, and great delights. Most of all it's Jesus' home, and it's a place where we'll feel right at home, a place where there's no more crying, or pain, or sorrow."

"It sounds much better than here," Littlefoot sniffed.

A soft whisper vibrated out of Elizabeth's parched lips, and Brannon bent low to hear her words.

"What did she say? Did she hear us? Can she talk?" Littlefoot almost shouted.

"She asked," Brannon smiled down at Elizabeth, "who the other two women were."

"What two women?"

"Oh, I guess she heard me say she was one of the two or three prettiest women I've ever seen, and she wanted to know the others. Well, my Lisa, of course. Of all women who have white skin, she was the most beautiful. And then there's a Spanish lady . . . you met her, Littlefoot — Señora Pacifica. Her Latin beauty captures the hearts of most every man that meets her. But, Elizabeth, you are the fairest of all the Indian maidens."

She motioned for Littlefoot to lean close. Then she whispered something to him. She tried to lift her hand to touch his face but didn't have the strength. He held his mother's hand and pressed it to his cheek.

"Mother says that I will have to take care of you because you are losing both your eyesight and your memory."

Brannon held her in his arms, and Littlefoot continued to press his hand against her cheek.

"I have sent for the doctor. Perhaps he can — "

Suddenly she reached up and pressed her fingers against his lips to silence him. They felt bony and very cold. Without considering the propriety of the act, Brannon kissed her fingers. Then, embarrassed, he took her hand in his and began to rub some of his warmth into it.

Her eyes were beginning to cloud and were fixed on the ceiling. He was sure she couldn't see anything at all.

"You are breaking our hearts . . . mine and Littlefoot's."

"Yes," she whispered, "I know . . ." Then she struggled to catch her breath. "I am grateful to the Lord that Littlefoot has someone to share his sorrow. To bear such grief by one's self will crush a person . . . unless they are as strong as The Brannon. He has always carried much sorrow alone."

Lord, I'm full . . . loaded down . . . exhausted . . . no more . . . no more sorrow. It will crush me!

"I am sorry I did not get to see your ranch. Do you think we will be able to look down from Heaven and see things on earth?"

"I . . . eh . . . I don't really know . . . but," Brannon added, "I don't suppose we will want to anyway."

"I will want to," she whispered.

In the distance he heard two shots ring out through the night. He started to lay her head

177

back down, then relaxed, and held her tight as he looked into her frightened eyes.

Read? He should have been back. Trevor! Lord, there's murder in the streets, and I can't do anything. Not Read . . . Lord, I can't bury another person. It's got to be someone else — not Read!

He held Elizabeth tighter.

"Mr. Brannon?" her faint voice now rattled in the chest. "I'm very cold."

He tucked the covers around her as he heard shouts and noises coming from the streets of Medicine Hat. He tried to peek out the back window of Hinson's Boarding House, but could see nothing but the break of a cloudy, gray dawn. He held her limp hand in his and began to rub it again.

"There . . . does that feel better?"

"I am very cold," she said again. "Hold my hand . . . please!"

"Mother, he is holding your hand," Littlefoot cried. "Oh, Mother, please . . . please don't die!"

Brannon moved his hand to one cheek, and Littlefoot placed his hand on her other.

"That is better," she whispered. "I am ready now. I am surrounded by the two bravest warriors I have ever known. They have both treated me with respect. It has been a good life."

Good life? Lord, it has been a horrible, miserable, pain-filled life for her! How can she say that? Lord, show her Your mercy. Show her Your great love!

He could feel the tears rolling down his cheeks.

"Mr. Brannon . . . he is now your son. I know you would have wished for your own boy to live . . . so I give you my son . . . Teach him to be brave. Teach him about our Jesus. Teach him to be proud of his mother."

Brannon quit trying to hold back the sobs. For twelve years he had tried to hold back the tears. For twelve years he had tried to hide all sorrow and grief. He could do it no longer. Like a wave on the gulf that rolls across the water for miles and finally crashes on the shore, the grief of lost loved ones shattered his emotions and his soul.

"Littlefoot . . . you have always been the delight of my heart. In a world that has not been kind, you have brought me great joy . . ."

She stopped and began to cough. Littlefoot looked at Brannon for assurance. He could almost feel the pain of each labored breath she took. Then, suddenly, she spoke with strength and clarity.

"Littlefoot . . . I did not have any choice in the matter about who your father would be. They held me down and forced that upon me. But if I had been allowed to choose . . . I would have chosen The Brannon. So when you treat him like your own father, you will be honoring me. And when he is old . . . it will be your turn to take care of him."

"I will, Mother . . . I promise, I will."

"And remember . . ." Her voice trailed off.

Brannon saw the pain in her face suddenly vanish; her eyes grew clear, and years seemed to melt away from her face.

"Remember what? Mother? Mother!"

"Oh . . . it is You! It is You! Lord Jesus, I knew You would come!" she cried.

The breathing stopped.

The ravages of the painful disease crept back into her face. Her cold body lay motionless and lifeless in Brannon's arms.

"Mother!" Littlefoot cried. He pulled her away from Brannon and hugged her to himself. "Mother!"

Brannon sat on the bed and stared.

Lord, take good care of her. And listen . . . if there are any rewards up there that you been saving for me, how about you giving some of them to Elizabeth? She deserves a little extra, Lord.

He had just wrapped his arms around Littlefoot and Elizabeth's body when the back door of the room banged open, and Marshal Young stormed into the room waving a shotgun. Two other men scrambled in behind him, both toting cocked revolvers.

"Mister, you are under arrest for gunnin' down Deputy Reynolds! You go for a gun, and I'll kill you right where you sit!"

Brannon didn't flinch.

Neither did he release Littlefoot or Elizabeth.

"Marshal, I don't know how many dumb things you've done in your life, but this has got to be the dumbest! Is Reynolds dead?"

"Not yet, but the doctor is trying to remove the bullets now. Lucky for him it happened right at the doctor's front door."

"Let me tell you something. Reynolds is a fine man, and I pray to God Almighty he pulls through. He was going over there to fetch the doctor for me. He had graciously allowed me, under his supervision, to come be with Elizabeth during her dying hours."

"He wasn't supposed to do that! There are rules about prisoners!"

"Well, Marshal, just in case you haven't heard, there are higher laws than those of the city of Medicine Hat. God's laws of decency, and mercy, and kindness. Reynolds was following a higher law."

"You ain't talkin' your way out of this. Haul him out of here, boys!"

"Marshal, the boy's mother has just died! She passed away in my arms while I waited for Reynolds to return with the doctor. I don't even have a gun. Mine is still locked in a drawer in your desk. If you have any scrap of decency, let us mourn her death in peace. Then I'll walk with you down to the jail. Let me have some time with the boy, and let me make arrangements for her."

"I told you before," the marshal barked, "you are going to jail! Boys, haul him off."

Brannon glanced up and saw one of the deputies look over at the other.

"You might as well shoot me right now, because I'm not going," Brannon informed them.

"Arrest him!" the marshal shouted.

"I ain't goin' to do it," Deputy Groten finally said.

"It ain't right, Marshal," the other spoke. "Every man has a right to mourn his kin."

The marshal raised his shotgun and stared at Brannon for a long time. Finally, he lowered the gun.

"You're right, boys . . . you're right. I was just upset about Reynolds. We'll give them some time."

NINE

An hour later they laid Elizabeth's lifeless body back on the feather bed and pulled the covers over her. Brannon looked up at the two deputies who watched over him. "I'm going to need to stop by an undertaker's and make some arrangements," he announced.

"We can't let you wander around town on your own."

"I figured you would come with me."

"Marshal said not to let you out the door without wrist irons," one of the men reminded him.

"If that's the way it's got to be . . . then let's do it." Brannon held out his hands as Groten locked on the shackles. Looking up, Brannon noticed Mrs. Hinson standing in the hallway with a dark green bathrobe wrapped around her. Her graying hair was pulled back tight behind her head.

"I knew it! I didn't want to rent to them! Look at that. It's just like I said. The man's a convict, and the woman's . . . my word! She's dead . . . there's a dead woman in my boarding house!"

"Yes, ma'am." One deputy nodded.

"Wait!" she called. "Wait! Come back here! What about the body? You aren't going to leave it here, are you? Come back here. What about this Indian? Who's going to . . ."

Brannon turned and stared at the woman, who suddenly grew silent as she caught the expression in his eyes.

"Mrs. Hinson," he advised, "I am on my way to the undertaker. He will be arriving here shortly. Until that time, close the door, and go about your business. Do not disturb the body. I cannot begin to describe the wrath I would feel if you were to behave in any manner less than Christian over this matter. Do you understand me?"

With mouth gaping, she nodded her head.

Most of the shops and stores in Medicine Hat were beginning to open when they walked out into the sunlight of a partly cloudy morning. Clerks and customers milled on raised wooden sidewalks. Freight wagons were unloading in the dirt streets which showed puddles from the rainstorm of the previous night. Heavy clay soil stuck to Brannon's boots. But the clean, cool air refreshed his lungs and lightened the burden of Elizabeth's death.

Lord, they're all going about their business as if nothing has happened. The world stops still for some, but rushes on for all the rest.

Howard LaFeete's Mortuary was located just across from the Bank of Utah. A crowd gathered as the bound man was marched by gunpoint to the undertakers. Littlefoot walked close by his side.

The funeral parlor was closed when they arrived, and one of the deputies scurried off to find the proprietor. With the wooden sidewalk packed with gawkers, Brannon and Littlefoot slumped onto a bench and waited.

"I hear he killed the marshal."

"No, it was Reynolds. He killed Deputy Reynolds."

"Is he picking out his own coffin?"

"Did you hear what happened over at the Hinson? Someone got killed over there too."

"Ought to string him up — that's what we should do. A man like that ain't fit for our world, no, sir!"

"I hear he's another one who claims to be Brannon."

"Like to see the real Brannon show up. I bet you this old boy wouldn't have a chance with the real Brannon."

"I seen him once."

"The real Brannon?"

"What's he like?"

"Big man . . . six-foot-five, he is. Sandy hair and muscles like a horse. No, sir, this old boy is a sorry specimen compared to the real Brannon."

Ignoring the voices, Brannon talked softly to Littlefoot. "Son, you'll need to wait with me at the marshal's office. The judge will be comin' in today, and I'm sure we'll get it straightened away."

"What about Mother?"

"Well, this man will fix her up nice . . . then we'll load her in the wagon and take her to Arizona to bury. She wanted to be at the ranch, so that's where she'll be. Is that all right with you?"

"Will I be able to visit her grave often?" the boy asked.

"You can go up there every day of the year if you want."

"I think . . . I think I will do that."

Brannon attempted to put his left arm around the boy's shoulders, but the wrist chains prevented him. He sighed deeply and looked up at the parting crowd on the sidewalk. Deputy Groten pushed his way through, leading a man in a dark suit and silk hat. The man fumbled to unlock the front door of the mortuary and then turned to Brannon.

"I wasn't expecting business so early." Then looking at the crowd, he continued, "I certainly hope you haven't stirred me out for a task I will be unable to perform."

"I presume you are not as narrow and bigoted as some of the others," Brannon interjected. "But I would like for this to be a private discussion."

The man signaled him to come inside the building. Brannon, Littlefoot, and both deputies followed the undertaker inside while an assembly of faces hovered about the windows in front of the store. He motioned for them to be seated and placed himself in a leather chair behind a neatly organized cherrywood desk.

The room was paneled in dark wood and had what Brannon thought was a peculiar, medicine-like odor.

"Now just what can I do for you?"

"The boy's mother, who happens to be a very good friend of mine, just died down at the Hinson house. I wanted to hire your services."

"The boy's mother? I presume she is Indian?"

"Obviously."

"Well, you see Mr. . . . uh, I don't believe I caught your name."

"Brannon. Stuart Brannon."

"Well, Mr. Brannon . . . say, you aren't the real . . . I mean . . . oh, of course not. As I was saying, I would like to accommodate you, but it is customary not to . . . well, normally the Utes take care of their own dead. You know they have tribal customs and — "

"She's not Ute; she's Nez Percé. And she's not with her people; she's with me. Now I'm willing to pay good cash dollars for your services."

"I'm afraid you don't understand. I cannot work with Indians."

"Let me get this right," Brannon fumed. "There's not enough mercy or kindness in the town of Medicine Hat to let a lady be buried with dignity?"

"It's not a question of kindness, I assure you," the man explained. "For me, one customer is certainly as good as another. But look out there . . . you see all those folks staring in? Well, if I start working with Indians, I'm liable not to

187

get one customer from the white folks. Do you know what that means? It means I go broke and lose the business, and my family goes hungry. It is not a moral decision. I simply cannot destroy my business."

"Any business based on hatred isn't worth keeping," Brannon retorted. "Look, I don't want a burial, nor a hearse, nor any public display. I just want you to prepare the body and place it in a coffin. Then if you'll keep it in your back room until I'm ready to pull out, I'll be taking the body to Arizona for burial. I'll pay you a fair price for your work."

"I'm afraid it's impossible . . . you see — "

"Why is it impossible?" Littlefoot questioned.

"What?"

"How about you explaining why you can't help us to the boy? This is the lady's only son. So go ahead, Mister. Tell him why you can't spare any compassion."

"Well . . . it's not a matter of compassion. Of course, son, I would like to . . . but, as I said earlier . . . I, eh, find it . . . you see, a person can't just . . . well . . ."

Littlefoot rubbed the sleeve of his shirt across his nose and glared at the man.

Howard LaFeete stood up, walked over to a hat rack, put on his round silk hat, took it back off, replaced it on the peg, walked halfway back to his desk, paused, and peered down at Littlefoot. Then he walked over to the others and sat down.

"You're right, Mister. If you can't stay in business doing what is right, then why be in business at all? I'll do it."

Brannon's face broke into a very slight smile. "Thanks, it's much appreciated."

"Now about those arrangements —," the man began.

"Here's what I want," Brannon explained. "You take special care to embalm that body to the best of your profession. We'll be on the road for a while, and I don't want any decay. Leave her dressed in that beaded deerskin and the moccasins next to the bed. Fix her up as nice as you can. Her hair ought to be braided in two pigtails and laying across her shoulders. She's not much over thirty, so if you can do anything to make her look her age, that would be much appreciated. Then I want you to lay her in a good quality, hardwood box on some white satin. As I said, I'll pick up the coffin just as soon as I've got this matter with the marshal cleared up."

"All right, I think I have all of that," the undertaker replied.

Brannon stood to his feet. "I'd shake hands on the deal, but it looks like they want to keep the chains on me."

"Eh . . . one other thing," Howard LaFeete added. "I'm sure you understand that . . . well, being a stranger in town and under your present condition . . . I'll need some payment in advance. No offense intended."

"Sounds reasonable to me." Brannon nodded. "Littlefoot, dig an eagle out of my pocket."

The boy jammed his hand down Brannon's duckings and pulled out a gold coin.

"I presume twenty dollars will cover things?"

"Yes, sir! Thank you . . . and," the man continued, "do you mind terribly if I showed you out the back door?"

The marshal sat at his desk reading some papers when they returned to the jail. The deputy unlocked the shackles and led Brannon to a cell.

"Marshal," Brannon asked, "when can I talk to the judge?"

"Judge sent word that the huntin's good, and he won't be home until Friday."

"Friday? What about due process? You can't hold me that long on unsubstantiated charges."

"Mister . . . I can hold you as long as I want to. Obviously, you're used to gettin' your way, but not here. Now you might be surprised to know that I sent a telegram like you suggested."

"To the governor of Arizona?"

"Nope. To the state prison in New Mexico. It seems that one Paul "Trevor" Nisqually was released from prison on June 6, 1888, after successfully completing his sentence."

"They let him out on purpose?"

"He served his time."

"Doesn't it concern you that he was sent to

jail for killing a sheriff?" Brannon demanded.

"What concerns me is my deputy was gunned down, and you're the most likely suspect."

"Did you ask Reynolds? Is he conscious? Ask him. He'll tell you!" Brannon urged.

"The deputy's recovering from serious wounds. He is unavailable for interrogation."

"Interrogation? Just go ask who shot him. For heaven's sake, Marshal, you've got to do that much."

"You know, Mister, you are the most arrogant man I've ever met. You spend the entire day telling me and my deputies what we can and cannot do. Reynolds is with his family now, and I have no intention of disturbing him until after dinner."

The marshal stood and reached for his hat. "Boys, I'm bushed. I'll be at home for a while. Don't take any gaff from this hombre, and don't let him out of the cell. Is that clear?"

The deputies nodded and waited for the marshal to leave. Then the one named Groten stirred the fire in the pot-bellied stove and set a pot of water on it. He scooped out a big handful of Arbuckles and poured it in the top and then replaced the lid.

"Deputy," Brannon called, "can the boy pull a chair over here and sit by me? He's a little upset over his mama."

"Shoot, I don't care if he sits in there with ya." The man opened the cell, and Littlefoot scooted inside.

"Much obliged." Brannon nodded.

"Say . . . I think I remember that incident about some guy named Trevor shootin' a sheriff," the man commented. "Where did that happen?"

"Over in Tres Casas, New Mexico. Up near the Colorado border."

"Yeah, that's the one. How did the real Brannon capture that old boy anyway? Did they shoot it out in the street, or what?"

"Nope," Brannon answered, "it was in a blacksmith's shop. Trevor jumped a pony and made tracks for the door, and I shot the horse out from under him."

"I'm surprised that a man like Brannon would shoot the horse."

"Why's that?"

" 'Cause a man like that would have killed Trevor on sight. Why do you suppose he blasted the horse? Maybe he squeezed off a bad shot."

"What if Brannon is a man who tries to avoid killing anyone?"

"But I've read them stories . . . Brannon has killed hundreds of men."

"Groten, did you know all those stories are made up by some New York City writer?"

"They ain't true?"

"Not a one of them."

"Well, I'll be! So old Brannon captured Trevor and turned him over to the law?"

"Nope. I captured Trevor and got appointed sheriff myself."

"Say . . . did you ever know a bartender in Tres Casas named LaVerne?"

"He worked at the Lavender Slipper, as I recall. I kind of got roughed up in that place. I took on four of them, and, well . . . I guess I sent them on down the road. Groten, how did you know LaVerne?"

"I'm his brother."

"You are? Well, where is he? He could identify me and —"

"LaVerne's dead. Took four bullets in the back one night up in Telluride."

"Did he ever mention what happened in Tres Casas?"

"Yep."

"Did I call it true?"

"Yep."

"So now do you believe me that I'm Stuart Brannon?"

"Nope."

"Why not?"

"'Cause *I* knew all of that, and I sure ain't Brannon."

The front door banged open with such force that all inside the marshal's office jumped to their feet. A winded man with black garters on his white cotton shirt sleeves raced in.

"Where's Marshal Young? The bank's been robbed! He shot Silverstein dead and grabbed the greenbacks!"

The deputies pulled rifles off the wall and grabbed boxes of bullets from the desk.

"Groten," Brannon called, "if it's Trevor, you watch out for him. He's got a sneak gun in his boot, and he doesn't mind popping you in the back!"

The deputy spun back. "You really are Brannon, aren't you?"

"Yep."

"I'll be . . . kind of wish you was out here helpin' us find this hombre."

"That makes two of us."

"Well," the deputy said with a shrug, "with any luck we won't find him until after you're out."

Both men ran out and left the wooden door banging.

"They left us?" Littlefoot asked.

"They'll be back."

"What about Mother? When will we get out of here?"

"I figure if Reynolds pulls through, maybe now he will testify as to who I am."

"And if he dies?" Littlefoot asked.

"I don't want to talk about that."

"It's like your toe."

"What?"

Littlefoot looked down at Brannon's new boots. "You don't want to talk about it either. Maybe you should pull off your boot and rest your toe."

"Nope."

"Why not?"

"It's getting so swollen now I wouldn't be

able to put the boot back on."

"How did you break your toe?"

"It doesn't matter how; it's just — "

"I'd like to know," Littlefoot insisted.

"It was nothing . . . really," Brannon replied. "I sure hope that old boy does a decent job with your mother."

"Did a woman really injure it like Red Shirt said?"

"No . . . it was nothing. I kicked a door — that's all. I was barefoot. Must have caught the big toe and bent it back until it broke. That's all there is to it."

"What door?"

"It doesn't matter," Brannon insisted.

"What door?" Littlefoot pressed.

"Look," Brannon said with a shrug, "I accidently kicked the outhouse door . . . okay? It was dark and I was in a hurry."

"After you kicked the door, then what happened?"

"I yelled and . . . and . . ."

"And what?"

"And . . . I got a little mad and shot the door."

Littlefoot's eyes grew big. "You did what?"

"Look, I blasted the door. That's all. It needed a little ventilation anyway."

"Well, ain't this a pretty sight? The so-called Arizona legend locked in a cell talkin' about shootin' outhouses!"

Trevor towered in the doorway, a revolver pointed at Brannon, his stovetop black boots pulled over the outside of his trousers. He constantly glanced back toward the street.

"The mighty Stuart Brannon sittin' in a jail cell. Sort of like ducks on a pond, ain't it?"

"Trevor!" Brannon grabbed toward a revolver that wasn't there. His eyes searched the cell as if he expected a gun to suddenly appear.

"This sight makes all those years almost worthwhile. Just one more shot, and my plans will be complete. Think I'll drift on up to Alaska after that now that the good citizens of Medicine Hat have handed me a little poke."

"He won't shoot us in jail, will he?" Littlefoot pleaded.

"Who, Trevor?" Brannon shoved Littlefoot behind him and stepped to the cell door. "Sure he'd shoot us in here. He sort of specializes in back-shooting or at least shooting unarmed men and boys. He doesn't have the courage to face me straight on."

"Save your breath, Brannon. You think you're talkin' to some kid? You ain't goin' to draw me out. Now won't that look good in the history books? 'Arizona legend, Stuart Brannon, dies in a jail cell in Utah!' Kind of reminds you of old Bill Hickok, doesn't it?"

"And what will the history books say about you? I suppose you'll be listed right there with Jack McCall. The mighty Trevor, he busted into jail houses and shot unarmed men and children. Yeah . . . your mama should be mighty proud of Paul 'Trevor' Nisqually!"

"Where did you get that name? It don't matter, Brannon. You're dyin' right there in a jail cell, and I don't give two cents what you or anyone else thinks."

"Yeah, that's what I just said. Take a good look at him, son. Most times you got to crawl on your belly to see someone like this."

Trevor's face flushed, and he rushed toward the cell.

Lord, save Littlefoot!

He reached behind him to push the boy under the heavy wooden bunk and suddenly felt the cool, slick grip of a revolver jammed into his hand.

Littlefoot had a gun all this time?

Talking loudly enough to cover the sound of the hammer cocking, Brannon called out, "That's it, Trevor . . . get a little closer. You wouldn't want to miss and hit the bars. A ricochet might come back and clip you. Besides, you aren't as good a shot as you used to be. Time will do that to a man . . . and you weren't all that good years ago!"

Brannon dove to the floor away from the bunk and Littlefoot. He and Trevor fired at the same time. Both bullets struck iron bars and flew wildly into the walls. Brannon shoved the barrel of the pistol through the bars and quickly pulled off a round that shattered into Trevor's right thigh.

At the same time Brannon rolled to the right and felt the vibration of two shots ripping the jail cell floor. Trevor dove out the door into the street, and Brannon's next shot splintered the doorway.

"Keep under there!" Brannon shouted to Littlefoot.

Brannon scrambled to find some protection from the next shot.

No shots came.

"Where is he?" Littlefoot called out.

"Stay down!"

"Did you kill him?"

Brannon aimed the Colt .44 at the front door.

"No . . . I clipped him in the leg. I didn't get a chance to aim any higher, but I sure didn't kill him."

Littlefoot pulled himself out from under the wooden bunk.

"Will he be back?"

"I don't think so . . . looks like people are gathering out in the street."

"I am glad I had that gun with me."

With an eye on the door, Brannon slipped an arm around the boy's shoulder and gave it a squeeze. "Well, it's like your mama said — we'll have to take care of each other now. Where did you get my spare gun?"

"Yesterday you told me to go back to the room and get the shotgun to protect Mother," the boy explained. "But the shotgun hurts my shoulder, so I dug a revolver out of your bedroll."

"Why didn't you mention it to me before Trevor walked in?"

"I was afraid you'd be mad at me for not doing what you asked . . . and . . . and I sort of forgot I had it. But when he came in waving that gun, I remembered."

"Brannon!" a voice yelled through the door. "This is the marshal. Have you got a gun in there?"

"Yep!" Brannon hollered. "And I'm glad you learned my name."

"Brannon, listen to me. I'm comin' through this door, and I want to see that gun lying on the floor. You got that?"

Brannon bent over and laid the gun in front of him.

"Okay, Marshal! Come on in!" Brannon shouted.

Marshal Young and Deputy Groten bolted into the room with guns drawn.

"How'd you get that gun?" the marshal asked.

"An angel brought it to me."

"Did you hit Trevor?" he asked, looking down at splashes of blood on the floor of his office.

"Yep. I winged him just above the right knee. He took off a moment ago, but I . . . eh, decided not to follow him. Did you make up your mind that I really am Stuart Brannon?"

"I don't have a lot of time to talk. We're rounding up a posse to find Trevor. As far as we can tell, he's headed south." He walked over and unlocked the jail cell.

"Groten, get Brannon his gun," he ordered.

"What made you change your mind about me?"

"Well, first off . . . when we got to the bank, three different men identified Trevor as the bank robber. That made me believe some of the things you been saying about him. Then when we were searching through town tryin' to find him, I stopped by to make sure Trevor didn't try to finish the job on Reynolds. Well, Read was able to tell me the truth and identify you as Brannon."

"Is he goin to pull through?" Brannon asked.

"Yeah . . . doc says he'll be laid up for a while, but he should do fine. Brannon," the marshal continued, "I don't suppose we could talk you into ridin' with us out after Trevor. You knowin' him like you do and with your reputation with a gun, we could use the help."

"Marshal, right now all Littlefoot and I want to do is get on the road back to the ranch with a wagon and a coffin. I'll have to decline your invitation."

"Well, we don't blame you none," the deputy chimed in. "Medicine Hat ain't exactly made you feel at home."

"In that case," the marshal continued, "I'll have to encourage you to leave town as soon as possible. I know it's not your fault, but we've had more crime and violence in the past two days since you came to town than we've had in the last six months."

"I'll be happy to oblige you, Marshal."

"You got any advice for following Trevor?"

"He's smart. And tricky. So figure out what

most men would do if they were in his condition. I can guarantee that Trevor will do something different. Keep together. Don't give him any breaks."

The marshal opened the top desk drawer and pulled out a couple of boxes of bullets. "We've got to ride. Sorry I can't officially escort you out of town."

"We can find our way out. And I pledge you, we'll leave as soon as the undertaker has finished his job."

The marshal and his deputy stomped back out the door and disappeared down the street. Brannon and Littlefoot just stood and stared at each other for a minute.

"Littlefoot, let's get out of this place!"

When they left the office, they saw several men loitering on the sidewalk.

"Mister, you really Stuart Brannon?"

"Yep."

"You the Brannon they wrote all them books about?"

"Yep."

"Did you do all those things that old boy writes about?"

"Nope."

"What do you mean?"

"He lied."

"Well . . . I'll swan . . . a bunch of lies."

Scurrying after them, another man hollered, "Who's that Indian kid? We don't allow no Indians to go . . ."

Brannon put his hand on the polished wooden grip of his revolver. "He's my son!"

"Oh . . . yes, sir . . . no offense, Mr. Brannon."

Brannon threw his arm around the boy's shoulder and cut across the muddy street. For the first time in a long time Brannon's mind was crammed with long-range plans for the future.

"How come you told them I was your son?"

"Well . . . the way I figure it, I'm as close to a father as you're going to get. And you're as close to a son as I'm going to get. You don't ever have to call me Father, but I just might call you son from time to time."

"I think that will be all right."

Brannon's first stop was to see Read Reynolds. Mrs. Reynolds ushered him into the house.

"Read always claimed to be a friend of Stuart Brannon's, but I just thought he was stretchin' it a bit," she confessed.

"Yes, ma'am . . . Read helped me out of a scrape on a train down near Tucson some years ago. How's he doing?"

"Well, the doctor says he should do all right with a lot of rest. Would you like to see him?"

"Yes, ma'am."

"Is this your son?" she asked pointing to Littlefoot.

The Indian boy looked up and smiled. "Yes!" he said.

Reynolds sprawled across a bed in a sparsely

furnished room next to the kitchen. The blankets were pulled halfway down, linen bandages were wrapped around his midsection, and a wet cloth lay on his forehead.

"Read, it's me — Brannon."

"Did they let you out, Mr. Brannon?"

"Only after Trevor took a couple shots at me."

"And he missed?"

"Yep. I was shooting back."

"You had a gun in jail?"

"Oh, yeah . . . the cell has all the modern conveniences."

"I hope you put some lead in him."

"A little."

"Good. There's a man who doesn't deserve to live."

"You might be right on that."

"Listen, Mr. Brannon . . . me and the wife been talkin'. As soon as I get my strength back, we're leaving Medicine Hat."

"I promised I'd help you find a job down in Prescott."

"I surely hope you don't take no offense at what I'm goin' to say . . . but every time I get around you, I end up gettin' shot. So we figure to go out to California where the wife's brother lives. A tiny old town called Visalia. It's in the big valley, you know? Maybe I'll do a little farmin'."

"Read, that's the best idea I've heard in two days. I'm headin' home myself. You all take care."

"Yes, sir, Mr. Brannon, I will. Say, do you suppose Mr. Hawthorne Miller will write about this one, too?"

"I wouldn't doubt it."

"Well, it sure do take a little of the sting out of being shot up, don't it?"

Brannon tipped his hat to Mrs. Reynolds and left with Littlefoot. It took them about an hour to get the wagon hitched, their horses out of the livery, and their belongings packed out of the boarding house.

Tossing the saddles into the wagon, they tied Dos Vientos and Six Bits to the back of the wagon and rolled up behind the undertaker's. LaFeete wasn't ready, so they stretched out in the wagon.

Littlefoot plopped down on a folded sheet of canvas. "Do you think about dying when you're in a gunfight?" he asked.

"Dyin'? Nope. I think about how to avoid getting shot and how to get the other guy to stop shooting. I do think about dyin'. But only when I have a lot of time to consider it proper."

At 11:45 A.M. they rumbled out of Medicine Hat, Utah, heading south toward the Arizona border.

An oak coffin, wrapped in a canvas, was securely tied in the back of the wagon.

TEN

The rainstorm had left the desert air so clean-tasting that every gulp seemed to lift Brannon's spirits. The soil, dried for months, had soaked up the precipitation as quickly as it fell. The road south out of Medicine Hat was wet enough that no dust trailed the wagon, yet no mud clung to the wheels.

Brannon handed the reins of the rig to Littlefoot who sat at his right.

"I have never driven a team," the boy admitted.

"You can do it. Just slap that line on the buckskin's rump if he starts getting lazy. The road looks straight for twenty miles."

Littlefoot jammed his boots against the footboard and watched the road intently. Without looking over at Brannon, he asked, "What will we do when we get to your ranch?"

"Our ranch," Brannon corrected.

"Yes . . . our ranch."

"Well, first we'll bury your mama. Then . . . I guess I haven't thought about it much. I suppose I'll have to see about getting you into a school."

"I am too old for school," Littlefoot announced.

"Too old? Who told you that?"

"In Florida we only went to school until we were twelve."

For the first time in days, Littlefoot's eyes relaxed. When he smiled, there was a sparkle in them, and he had a twist of the mouth that looked identical to his mother's.

Well, Elizabeth . . . he will always be your boy . . . and probably break a few young girl's hearts.

"I think you should get as much education as you can," Brannon lectured.

"How old were you when you quit going to school?"

"Eh . . . I guess about fifteen . . . but look at me. Why if I would have gone to school and maybe to one of those eastern colleges, I could be a . . ."

"An Indian agent?" Littlefoot offered.

"Eh . . . yeah, well . . . I don't guess everybody has to go to college. We'll get you more education, but we might have to wait 'til next spring. I hear they're trying to get a school started over at Big Butte. If they do, you could ride Six Bits over there."

Brannon reached back and pulled a leather pouch out of his belongings.

"There's a stage coming!" Littlefoot called.

"Just pull 'er to the right . . . that-a-boy . . . now slow down and let him by. And wave to the driver."

The stage rumbled past as the driver tipped his hat.

"Why do we wave to the driver?" Littlefoot asked.

"Because it's polite, and it shows friendly intent."

Littlefoot worked to find a comfortable rhythm with the team as he moved them back to the middle of the road.

"Are you going to clean the guns?" Littlefoot quizzed as he watched Brannon pull a wire and some small rags out of the leather pouch.

"Yep."

"Are you expecting a fight?"

"Nope."

"Then why are you doing that?"

" 'Cause when I need 'em . . . I'll need 'em clean. You doin' okay, or do you want me to take over?"

"I think I'd like to do this for a while. Where do you suppose that man Trevor is?"

"Halfway to Mexico, I suppose. But he'll have to find a doc to wrap up that leg. It was bleeding fairly heavy."

"Will he come after you?"

"Nope . . . I don't think so. I don't think he wants a face-to-face fight. And now, with a busted leg and plenty of money, he'll ride for the border."

"Will he come back someday?" Littlefoot continued to question.

"I suppose . . . he seems to be intent on proving something. Provided he doesn't get himself killed first."

"Does that frighten you?"

"You mean, having Trevor on the prowl? Well, no . . . I guess I sort of live with that all the time. It doesn't really scare me."

"It does not frighten me either," Littlefoot announced. Then he looked over at Brannon as he cleaned one of the Colts. "Will I get to wear a gun on my hip also?"

Brannon grabbed the boy by the back of his neck and tousled his hair. "Not yet. You don't want to start wearing a sidearm."

"Why?"

"Because then someone will force you to use it. When that happens, you either die, or you get a reputation. And it's a reputation that makes you keep on wearing it. It's a violent cycle. The best thing is to never get started. Besides, this land is changing. It's settling down. The time will come when the only reason to wear a Colt will be to shoot rattlesnakes."

"Do I get a rifle of my own?"

Brannon rubbed the stubble of his week-old beard.

"I've got a nice carbine that ought to fit you just right. We'll have to go hunting this fall, after the roundup."

"Roundup?" Littlefoot pressed.

"In the fall we bring down the cows and calves that have been . . ." Brannon studied the boy's questioning eyes. "Don't worry about it now. You've got plenty of time to learn the cattle business."

"Will you teach me everything?"

Littlefoot didn't notice that Brannon had turned his face aside and brushed his shirt across his eyes.

I've been waiting years to teach a boy how to ranch!

"Yep . . . I reckon you'll learn more than you ever wanted to." Brannon smiled.

The road was basically flat, with an occasional dip into a dry arroyo or a rise over low desert hills. Brannon listened closely. He couldn't tell if the slight squeak was a wheel that needed greasing or merely part of the ringing in his ear that had been present since their gun battle at the valley of the chimneys.

Littlefoot looked over at Brannon and blurted out, "Which bunk is going to be mine?"

With his mind reliving that morning's gun battle with Trevor, Brannon stammered, "Bunk . . . what?"

"At the ranch . . . you and me and Mr. Andrews slept in bunks. Can I have the one by the door?"

"Oh . . . bunk. You don't get to sleep in a bunk."

Brannon could see the worry in Littlefoot's eyes.

"I don't?"

"Of course not. I'm not going to let you sleep in the bunkhouse with Billy and Pete."

"You aren't?"

"Nope. You'll have to sleep in the big house

with me. You can have that bedroom next to the kitchen."

"I can?"

"It's all yours. 'Course we might want to change the fixin's some. I built that room for . . . it was to be a . . . I mean, for the baby. Anyway, that's your room. Remember, you aren't a hired man. That means you can't quit me, and I can't fire you. You got that?"

"I really get to live in the mansion?"

Brannon peeked over at Littlefoot. The boy's teasing eyes gleamed.

"The mansion? Well, I've never heard anyone call it that before."

"You should have seen how small our homes were in Florida."

"I don't want to even think about it. Now do you want to crawl back there and take a siesta?"

"I am not tired," Littlefoot asserted.

"Well, I am . . . so you keep her on the road, and we'll go a couple more hours before we stop for a rest. I'm going to catch a little nap. If you need anything, holler."

Sometimes in the warm softness of his bed at the ranch, Brannon would lie awake at night staring at the ceiling. On those nights, nothing he would do seemed to help him sleep. His bones could ache; his mind could be exhausted, and yet it raced from one idea to another, unable to relax. He would go out and check on horses that didn't need him. Or he'd warm some milk, and then not like the taste of it. Or pull down his worn black Bible and do a little reading. Or just lie there trying to figure how to store more spring runoff in his holding ponds.

But he wouldn't . . . couldn't sleep.

Not even if he threw his bedroll down in the front yard or stretched out in the hayloft. At times like that absolutely nothing helped.

This was not one of those times.

This time Brannon knew he could fall asleep in the middle of the main street of Tucson with a fiesta in progress.

The wagon rattled, bounced, squeaked. His sore foot slammed occasionally into the wooden side boards. His head banged into the seat or the cantle or even the horn of his saddle.

It didn't matter.

He slept soundly.

A shout finally stirred him.

A deep, harsh, threatening shout.

When Brannon opened his eyes, he thought it was dark. Then he realized that the tarp that had covered Elizabeth's coffin had jiggled off and engulfed him. In the darkness he pulled his revolver.

The wagon's stopped!

"I didn't ask you if you wanted to sell them horses. I said, we're buying those horses. Ten dollars each — that's a fair price for Indian ponies. Ask any of these men."

Kicking off the canvas, Brannon jumped to his feet on the back of the wagon. Towering over what he discovered to be three men on horseback, he cocked the revolver and pointed it at the spokesman.

"You wranglin' with my boy?" he demanded.

Dropping his mouth as if seeing the dead rise, the spokesman stammered, "Well, I'll be . . . eh . . . Mister, we was just tryin' to buy some horses, that's all!"

"Yeah," another of the men added, "we didn't know anyone was alive . . . I mean, we saw the coffin and — "

The third man interrupted, "Say, ain't you . . . I mean, you sort of look like — "

"He's Stuart Brannon," Littlefoot informed them.

"We're dead, Leon!" the man moaned, holding his hands up. "I told you to leave the boy alone!"

"Mr. Brannon . . . Mr. Brannon, we ain't meanin' no harm," the spokesman insisted. "We offered a fair price . . . I mean, those are fine horses, and sometimes them Injuns . . . eh, those Indian boys are out selling horses. It was an honest mistake."

Brannon kept the gun pointed at the man. "You were trying to cheat this boy out of two horses he didn't want to sell."

"Oh, no, sir, we —," one of the other men

began. Quickly Brannon turned the gun to that man. "Oh," the man blurted out, "you're right . . . that price was too low. No, sir, we probably cain't afford them fine horses. So we'd like to just mosey along, if you don't mind, sir."

"You don't plan on going down the road cheating Indian boys, do you?" Brannon asked.

"No, sir, Mr. Brannon!"

"Well . . . that's better." Brannon slipped the revolver back into the holster, then reached down, and grabbed his canteen. Taking a big gulp, he looked around at the desert scenery. "It sure is a mighty pretty day, isn't it?"

"Eh . . . yes, sir, it . . . it is," one of them responded.

"You boys need a drink of water?"

"Well . . . eh . . . I could use one," the oldest of the three admitted.

Brannon tossed him the canteen. "Help yourselves. It's a good ride yet before you get to Medicine Hat."

After taking a long drink and handing the canteen to his compadres, the man asked, "Mr. Brannon . . . you going to a funeral?" He pointed at the oak casket.

"Yep. The boy's mother passed on, and we'll be burying her at the ranch. Did I introduce you to my son, Littlefoot?"

"Yer son? Stuart Brannon has a son?"

"I ain't never heard that before," another exclaimed.

"Well, you heard it now." Brannon climbed up

to the wagon seat and took the reins from Littlefoot.

"Yes, sir, we certainly have." The third man rode over and handed the canteen back to Brannon.

"Thanks for the water. And . . . eh . . . thanks for not comin' out of that wagon throwin' lead."

"Don't think another thing about it . . . but I'll tell you right now you will live a little longer if you don't go around hassling lads."

"No, sir, I don't suppose we'll try that again. Good-bye, Mr. Brannon!"

"Good-bye, boys."

The three turned and rode north over the next bluff.

"How come you did that?" Littlefoot questioned. "They were going to steal our horses."

"They weren't going to steal 'em, but they were trying to cheat you. It's a whole lot better to make friends instead of enemies. And shooting people . . . well, that's the absolute last resort . . . when they don't give you any other choice." Then turning and looking at Littlefoot, he asked, "Are you all right? Why didn't you wake me up?"

"I did, didn't I? Besides, I didn't need any help." Littlefoot shrugged. "They weren't really going to shoot. I could see it in their eyes . . . couldn't you?"

"Well, yeah . . . but I didn't . . ." Brannon stalled. "Anyway, I didn't know I was that tired. Maybe you'd like to rest awhile."

"I like driving the wagon," Littlefoot reported.

"Then go ahead. Let's roll it up to that cliff on the right. We need to park awhile and rest the horses."

"Over by the mountains?"

"Yep."

"That's way off the road."

"But it looks like the only shade until the sun drops lower. Besides, I think we just might be close to Arizona now. That means we ought to make Mexican Wells by tomorrow evening, and maybe the ranch a couple of days after that."

Littlefoot drove the wagon near the cliffs and stopped it in the shade. Brannon, now sitting on Littlefoot's right, reached back to lift his Winchester rifle out of the wagon. As he did, the walnut stock of his rifle exploded with a shower of splinters, and an echo from a gunshot rang down from the cliff.

He immediately threw his right arm around Littlefoot. Both tumbled into the back of the wagon as the second shot ripped through the seat where they had just been sitting, flinging splinters and wood chips into the horses, which panicked and stampeded across the desert floor.

"Who shot at us?" Littlefoot yelled.

"I don't know, but we've got to stop this team!" Brannon yelled, crawling back over into the wagon seat. The leather lead lines dragged in the dirt under the wagon, and both horses showed no signs of slowing. The wagon bounced with such violence that Brannon feared it would tip over at any moment.

He tried to reach down and snag the reins, but he could stretch no more than halfway to the ground.

"Cut the saddle horses loose!" he yelled.

"What?"

"Get your knife and cut the lead ropes on Dos Vientos and Six Bits."

"I don't have a knife," Littlefoot screamed back.

Reaching into his pocket, he tossed a buckhorn folding knife to the boy. "Cut them loose before they hurt themselves!"

Brannon hung one leg over the now-shattered wagon seat and thrust his whole body over the edge of the wagon. Holding on with his left leg and his left hand, he lowered his body toward the desert floor which seemed to be flying by underneath him.

His foot started to slip, and he held on with his left hand even tighter.

Lord, I have no intention of leaving Littlefoot an orphan! I surely hope that You agree.

In the sunlight beside the wagon he saw Dos Vientos race by, and he knew that Littlefoot had released the horses.

Just a little more — if I can hook my toes, maybe I could . . .

As the fingers on his right hand dragged the dirt and scooped up the reins, his left boot slipped off the seat, and he could feel himself start to fall.

"No, not yet!" he bellowed.

Suddenly Littlefoot reached over the side of the wagon, threw both arms around Brannon's left knee, and held on.

Brannon jammed the salty, dirty reins between his teeth and clutched the rail with both hands. With Littlefoot's help he fell back into the wagon and grabbed the reins in his hands.

"There's a rider behind us!" Littlefoot cried out.

"How many?"

"One."

Brannon heard a whistle above his head and the report of the rifle at the same instant.

He's trying to shoot the horses! It's Trevor!

Another shot whizzed past them, and he shoved Littlefoot low into the wagon. At the same time he was trying to gain some control of the team. They failed to slow down at all, but he did get them to veer off to the right and then back to the left, dodging bullets.

"Shoot him!" Littlefoot hollered out. "Why don't you shoot him?"

"Couldn't hit him with the Colt, and the Winchester's broken!" Brannon yelled.

"Where's the shotgun?" Littlefoot screamed.

Brannon could feel the team beginning to come under control, and at the same time the rider was gaining on them.

"He's too far away. Hang onto that coffin. we're turning up that gulch!"

Just as they dipped down into a dry wash, Brannon turned the rig hard right, and two wheels lifted off the ground. Standing and leaning his body to the right, he could feel the wheels crash back to the ground.

At the same moment he heard the distant rifle fire and instantly felt something cut his arm. His shirt sleeve ripped away, and blood streaked from below his elbow down to his right wrist.

"You're shot!" Littlefoot cried.

"It's okay . . . I think it's just a ricochet. The bullet was spent!"

"Look at that horse!"

Brannon looked up to see the left horse bleeding from the neck.

"Well, maybe it wasn't completely spent! Take these reins!"

Littlefoot grabbed the leathers and held tight.

"Drive it up this wash and then cut left into the desert!"

"What are you going to do?"

"Get rid of this malo hombre! Keep it rolling!"

The horses were starting to tire, especially pulling up the grade. Brannon looked back and noticed that the gunman was blocked from sight for a moment as he descended into the arroyo. Grabbing his revolver in his left hand, Brannon dove from the wagon toward some sage that lined the dry creekbed. Then, rolling to a stop against the bank, he spun the cylinder and shoved another cartridge into the chamber.

I'm going to need all six this time!

His right arm, now covered with dust and dirt, felt as if it were lying on a hot stove. He held the gun in his left hand and hopelessly waved his right arm as if to cool it off.

Hearing the horse approach, he holstered the gun and grabbed two handfuls of dry gravel. As the rider came close, he tossed the gravel at the horse's face and retrieved the Colt out of his holster.

The gunman fired the rifle once wildly in Brannon's direction. The man's horse, spooked by the sudden gun blast as well as the gravel, reared up, tossing the man to the dry creekbed. The rifle tumbled off to the front of the horse. Brannon had one knee on the man's chest and a gun to his head before the man could catch his breath.

"Trevor! You just won't give up, will you?" Brannon panted. He reached into Trevor's holster for his Colt and tossed it aside. Then he searched the gunman's boots for the sneak gun and tossed it even further.

The gunman tried to say something but was gasping for air. He pointed for Brannon to move the knee off his chest. Just as Brannon started to comply, Trevor suddenly locked his hands together and drove them into the wound on Brannon's arm. The severe pain caused him to drop the revolver. Trevor reached to grab the gun, but Brannon kicked it hard across the ravine with his right boot.

The agony of the broken right toe crushing into the heavy revolver caused him to cry out, then stagger, and drop to his knees.

Trevor struggled to his feet, but the gunshot wound in his leg from the morning's battle at the Medicine Hat jail kept his kick from landing on Brannon's head. Instead, the worn boot caught Brannon in the shoulder, which knocked his arm out from under him. He slammed face first into the sand.

Shifting all his weight to his wounded leg, Trevor collapsed to the sand as well. He began to crawl toward Brannon's revolver which lay only a few feet away.

Grabbing the gunman's feet, Brannon dragged Trevor across the sand. The gunman wrenched loose and kicked hard at Brannon's shin. Brannon staggered as Trevor regained his feet.

All pain suddenly vanished from Brannon's mind, and he threw a punch at Trevor's nose that seemed to originate in his knees and whip right out his fist. Trevor barely had time to turn his head as the knuckles crushed into his cheekbone just below his left eye.

The impact made the sound of a bullwhip and sent Trevor crashing into the dirt on his back. Instantly Brannon felt all the misery magnified that had so miraculously subsided only seconds before. His whole right hand was tortured with pain, and he couldn't move his right arm at all. Holding that arm beneath him, he crawled on his knees and his one good hand toward his Colt, as he gasped for air.

Grabbing the wooden handle of the revolver with his left hand, he rolled back to face Trevor just as the gunman, still on his hands and knees, seized his two-shot sneak gun.

"Throw it down, Trevor!" Brannon yelled just as Trevor pulled the trigger.

The bullet slammed into the dirt not six inches from Brannon's right knee. Then both men shot at the same time.

Trevor's gun jammed.

Brannon's didn't.

The impact of the .44 hit Trevor in the center of the chest and tumbled him ten feet across the dry gulch.

Brannon started to cock the .44, but knew there was no need. He crawled toward Trevor. The pain in his own foot and arm made his progress slow. Reaching the gunman, Brannon rolled him over. He propped Trevor's head up on the dry creek bank. Brannon's eyes met the gunman's, but neither man spoke. Both gasped for air.

Brannon pulled his own bandanna off and folded it against Trevor's wound. Then he yanked the man's hand around and pushed it against the bandanna.

"You done killed me this time, Brannon!" Trevor choked.

"Yep. I reckon I did. You didn't give me any choice."

"How come you missed my heart?"

"I don't shoot too good left-handed anymore," Brannon panted.

"You're the luckiest man I ever met. My gun jammed. How come it was my gun that jammed?"

"Sneak guns aren't too reliable," Brannon offered.

"You're the best, Brannon. You're the best gunman I ever faced. I thought maybe the years would have changed you."

"We both grew older, Trevor. And if it does you any good, you're the best I ever faced."

"Are you stretchin' me?"

"Nope. And you know my word's good."

"I was pretty good, wasn't I?"

"Yep. I knew you'd always keep comin' after me. You should have been a sheriff somewhere, Trevor. You could have brought them all in."

"Sheriff? I'd have got shot in the back by some drunk."

He closed his eyes and coughed like a drowning man.

"You kept me from being the best for fifteen years. Just once . . . once I wanted to be the best there was. This is crazy . . ." He choked. "This is a crazy way to die!"

"Hatred and revenge have done in more men than any Indian tribe. Trevor . . . you need to settle things up with . . ."

Brannon's words faded as he looked down at the dead gunman.

Lord, it looks like the devil got another one. And, Jesus, I'm not really sure why it was me, instead of him, who got the last shot. But, Lord, I've got a boy to raise now. You know I don't know much about how to do that. But I can't be looking back wondering who's coming to gun me next. I surely do ask that this might be the last man I ever have to shoot.

Brannon lay back on the sand next to Trevor and tried to take deep breaths. He cradled his injured arm on his chest and glanced up at a clear blue desert sky. He thought he heard hoofbeats.

Trevor didn't have others with him . . . did he?

Too tired to sit up, he held the revolver in his left hand and waved it at the side of the arroyo. Suddenly Littlefoot, riding bareback, jumped Six Bits over the bank and into the dry stream bed. He held the shotgun across his lap.

"It's over!" Brannon called.

"Is he dead?"

"Yes."

"Are you shot?"

"I'm all right. Come help me up," Brannon called. Just as he struggled to his feet, several riders came into view on top of the gulch.

"Marshal Young!"

"Brannon? Did you get him?"

"Yeah . . . he's dead."

"How about the bank money?" one of the posse yelled.

"I have no idea about that . . . that's his

horse. You can check it out."

The men retrieved Trevor's body and helped Brannon out of the arroyo. He sent Littlefoot back to corral the wagon and Dos Vientos.

"Marshal!" Deputy Groten called out. "All the money's right here in the saddlebags!"

"Let's head home then, boys. We'll tie his body to that horse . . . unless Brannon wants to return to Medicine Hat with us. Then we could just toss him in the wagon."

"I've got no reason to go back there."

"Maybe you ought to let the doc fix up that arm." Groten motioned as he climbed back out of the gulch.

"You might want to return for the reward. The bank offered $200 for the return of the money," the marshal announced.

"Give it to Reynolds."

The marshal turned quickly and stared at Brannon. "What?"

"Give it to Reynolds and tell him to buy a nice little farm near Visalia."

"Where?"

"He'll understand."

"We'll tell him, Mr. Brannon," Groten assured him. "I guarantee we'll tell him. You headed on down to your ranch?"

"Yep."

"That boy can surely ride that pinto horse, cain't he?"

"Yep."

"He must get that from his pa, right?"

"Nope." Brannon stared across the desert where Littlefoot was driving the wagon back toward them. "I can guarantee you, he gets it all from his mother."

ELEVEN

By the time the posse pulled out on their return trip to Medicine Hat, Littlefoot had fetched the wagon and rounded up Dos Vientos. After catching his wind, Brannon checked on the horses and discovered the buckskin driving horse was not seriously wounded.

"What is in that little green bottle?" Littlefoot asked as Brannon pulled it from his belongings.

"Horse liniment . . . mainly just alcohol, I suppose."

"What are you going to do with it?"

"Help this old boy . . . I hope. Now you grab that buckskin's ear and give it a real hard twist."

"What?" Littlefoot questioned

"Twist that ear."

"Won't that hurt him?" Littlefoot quizzed.

"Yep. But it will get his mind off what I'm doing with his wound."

The big horse stood perfectly still as Littlefoot twisted his ear. Brannon poured about half the contents of the bottle on the animal's neck.

"Well . . . now it's my turn."

Littlefoot looked over as Brannon tried to roll

up his ripped and bloody right sleeve.

"You going to pour that on your arm?"

"Yep."

"Do you want me to twist your ear?" Littlefoot asked.

Brannon laughed into the teasing eyes of the boy. Pouring the liquid along the length of his wound, Brannon let out a roar that caused Littlefoot to jump.

"Are you all right?"

Catching his breath and brushing back some tears, Brannon choked out, "I never . . . felt better . . . in my life!"

He left his right sleeve rolled up above the elbow and carried his right arm close to his body, trying not to bump it. After securing the coffin under the canvas tarp, he retied the saddle horses to the back of the wagon, and checked the running gear on the driving horses. Finally they crawled back into the wagon.

Brannon motioned at the broken, bullet-riddled bench. We can't both sit up here anymore. You think you can drive this thing a while longer?"

"Yes."

"Well, I'll park back here on these saddles, and you drive it south. We'll camp on that last knoll right before we get to Mexican Wells."

The fiery pain in his right arm kept Brannon awake most of the night. Under the clear desert night sky, he made plans for the future.

He'll have to have at least a little more school-ing. I'll teach him how to brand next spring . . . maybe he could learn to shoe this winter, and he'll have to learn to carpenter . . . but he's still a kid!

He'll have to play and make friends . . . I suppose Earl and Julie's gang will be too young, but maybe in Prescott . . . 'course they might not like an . . . they'll have to like him; he's my son.

Sure hope Judge Quilici is feeling better. I'll have him tell me how to adopt the boy. While we're down there, I'll buy him some clothes, and . . . and whatever else a boy needs. Plenty of food ---- I can tell that already. Maybe it's about time to hire a cook. Billy and Pete wouldn't mind a decent meal either. I could build a little cookhouse and . . . 'course I wouldn't need it if I was married. With his skin color it would seem natural for him to belong to Vickie and me . . . but that won't ever . . .

Lord, life sure is easier when you're on your own. 'Course it's mighty lonesome too.

They rattled into Mexican Wells early the next morning to buy a few supplies and refill their canteens. Several men were digging a grave out behind the combination cafe, store, saloon, and livery — the only permanent build-ing in town.

Brannon and Littlefoot pushed open the tall door and peered inside the dark, smoky room.

"Say, we don't allow no . . . ," a voice from across the store began. "Oh, Mr. Brannon, is that you?"

"Yep. We need a few supplies, Riverton."

"Is that Injun with you?" The overweight, balding man in a dirty apron came into view.

"Yep."

"Oh, well . . . my . . . in that case . . ." the man stammered.

"Who's the funeral for?" Brannon quizzed. "Must have been one of your customers because this place looks deserted."

"Everyone's looking for the Lost Apache Mine."

"The what?"

"Well, that grave is for Thomas Stillwell."

"I don't believe I knew him."

The store owner gathered up items on Brannon's list as he continued the story, "Well, he was an old prospector that hit it rich and then couldn't find his diggin's. He got to be quite a bother out east of here. Always accused other folks of tryin' to steal his claim."

"I think I ran across him last week!" Brannon remembered.

"Well, sir . . . he came in here two days ago sportin' to have rediscovered the mine, plopped down a poke of gold that'd make any man smile. But this mornin', when I went to wake him, he was dead. Not shot or knifed, mind ya — just dead."

"So a few of you are burying him, and everyone else wants to go claim his mine?"

"You called it right. He kept talking about apeachies, which was the old man's way of saying Apaches. We figured it was down in a box canyon somewhere in Apache country. Say, if you seen him last week, did he mention a gold mine?"

"Do you think that old man would walk up to me and tell me where his gold mine was?"

"Eh . . . no, I guess not. No matter, I'm sure one of the boys will find it."

"As long as the Apaches don't find them first," Brannon added, gathering up his supplies.

"Ya know, it's a funny thing . . . old man Stillwell has been rantin' and ravin' for ages about his gold mine. Years ago he flashed some color around, but lately now he's been poorer than a Digger. Ain't that funny? He finally finds it, comes in here, and croaks! . . . Anything else, Mr. Brannon?"

"You have any ready-made britches and shirts for yearlings like this lad?"

"Ain't got much. You can check in that box over there and see what's left. Only got one size, but with some garters on the sleeves they should work."

When they left, Littlefoot wore new brown ducking britches, a white collarless cotton shirt (with sleeves held up by garters), black leather suspenders with silver conchos, a pair of black stovetop boots, and a wide-brimmed, black, beaver felt hat tilted to the side.

"How does it look? Do I look older?" he quizzed.

"Littlefoot, you look . . . at least fourteen," Brannon teased.

"Do I really? I feel older. Do you know I think this last week has made me feel older than any other week in my life."

"Yep, I know just how you feel." Brannon nodded. "There's just one thing missing from your hat."

"What's that?"

Brannon reached up to his own hat and tugged loose the worn eagle feather that lay matted against the horsehair hat band. "You need a genuine eagle feather. This one was given to me by Cholla. He's one of the leaders of a band of Apaches."

"I can put it in my own hat?"

"Yep."

"Now I will look like The Brannon!"

"Folks will more than likely get us mixed up," Brannon said laughing.

With the wagon in such poor repair, Littlefoot rode Six Bits south from Mexican Wells while Brannon drove the rig. He found himself answering a constant barrage of questions from Littlefoot about everything from past gun battles to how to break horses.

It was the second day out from Mexican Wells when the boy mentioned the subject of Señora Victoria Pacifica.

"She is really your girlfriend, isn't she?"

Brannon was busy scanning the horizon on a draw up ahead of them.

"Well . . . if we were young folks . . . I guess you might say that. We are good friends. We've both been through lots of tough times . . . and a few tough times together. But we surely don't get to see each other very much. I wish she lived closer."

"Are you going to marry her?" Littlefoot blurted out.

"What?" Brannon choked.

"I saw the way you kissed her good-bye at the ranch, and my mother told me I could not kiss anyone like that unless I was planning on marrying her."

"Your mother told you that?"

"Yes. And she told me much more about girls. She even told me some things I did not want to know," he admitted.

"Well . . . that's eh . . ." Brannon brushed back the sweat on his forehead and noticed that his hands were moist also. "I'm glad she told you those kinds of things. Now, as for me, well, I plan on teaching you how to — "

"You did not answer my question," Littlefoot interrupted.

"You mean, about marrying the Señora?"

"Yes."

"I surely have thought about it from time to time. I suppose if I ever did get married again, Vickie would be my choice."

"Why her?" Littlefoot insisted.

"She's an attractive, intelligent, creative woman who is very enjoyable to be around. She knows what it's like to go through difficult times, and she is very easy to talk to."

"I have been through difficult times," Littlefoot informed him. "And I am very easy to talk to."

Brannon pushed his hat back, scratched his neck, and slapped the lead line across the buckskin's rump. For several minutes neither spoke.

"I'm guessing that you don't want me to marry Victoria," Brannon finally said.

"I have never had a father, but now I have one," Littlefoot offered. "I think I like having a father. But I have a mother . . . she is gone, yes, but she will always be my mother. I would not know what to do with another mother."

"To be honest . . . I think you're pretty safe. The Señora and I are just a little too stubborn and independent to ever make up our minds about marriage. But from time to time we will go to the hacienda for a visit. Her brother, Ramon, is very good at breaking and riding horses. I imagine he would teach you a thing or two."

Littlefoot broke out in a big smile. "Did you say you are not marrying the Señora?"

"Not for a while anyway."

"Oh," Littlefoot shouted, "of course! When I am older and have my own wife, perhaps you could marry her then! You know, if you still wanted to have a friend."

"Thank ya, son. That's mighty kind of you," Brannon joshed.

"You are welcome." Littlefoot nodded, a smug smile on his face.

At noon the next day they rolled to the top of the north mountain pass leading down into Sunrise Valley and stopped the wagon. The day was clear and hot. Brannon's right arm still looked gruesome, but was starting to scab over. His toe felt fairly good as he drove the wagon, but it always made him limp when he walked.

But on the inside, Brannon hadn't felt this good in years.

"We got a little rain last week!" he reported, waving his finger toward the eastern mountains.

"How can you tell?"

"I can see water shimmering in the third catch pond up on the mountain. It was dry last week."

"Is that good?"

"Good! It's like manna from Heaven. Here's the first rule in ranching — always welcome the rain. Never turn it away at the door. Rain is your friend."

He took a big breath, slapped the lead lines, and rambled down the road toward ranch headquarters.

Lord, even in a dry season, that's just about the prettiest scene I ever saw. The home ranch is like a comfortable boot . . . nothing on earth ever feels so good as being back. Thanks, Lord . . . for my little piece of this old earth.

As they drew closer to the buildings, Brannon's mind wandered up the mountain to the upper ranges.

"Where's everyone?" Littlefoot called out.

"Oh . . . Billy and Pete will be moving the cows and calves down to that third pond we spotted from the pass. Won't be any of the others around. They all went home, and I had Tap send that telegram to — "

"No, I mean those horses over by the fruit trees. They weren't there last week." Littlefoot pointed to two gray horses picketed nearby.

"Well . . . I . . . eh, I didn't see 'em," Brannon sputtered. He reached back in the wagon for the shotgun. Cracking it open, he shoved in two shells and brought the wagon to a stop. "I'm certainly going to find out what's going on. You wait here!"

"Will there be more shooting?" Littlefoot asked.

"That's up to them, but I'm not putting up with hijacking at my own ranch," he stormed.

When he was halfway across the yard, the front door of his home opened. He started to raise the shotgun. Then he recognized the flashing dark eyes.

"*¿Señora? ¿Qué is este? ¿Por qué no va a su hacienda?*" Brannon quizzed.

Victoria Pacifica crossed her arms and

scowled. "Well . . . El Patron is finally home. Is your arm hurt badly?"

Two young men in store-bought suits stepped out on the porch behind her, drinking coffee. Neither appeared armed.

"This is El Patron?" one of the men asked. "What in the world does that mean?"

The other smiled and nodded at Brannon but mumbled under his breath, "This is the old man."

"My word! This is a complete surprise . . . no one told me!" Then he walked over to Brannon. "Been out huntin', have you, sir?" he asked.

"Yeah, you might say that. Just who are you two?"

"Well, I'm Ellis McKnight. I work for the *Sun* down in Phoenix. This is Mr. Goffley, a reporter from New York City. He happened to be in town and wanted to come along."

"What are you fellas doing out here?"

"Well, sir, we came to interview your son." The reporter smiled.

"My son?"

"Yeah, the famous gunman, Mr. Stuart Brannon."

"My son? Stuart Brannon?"

"Yes, sir. And if you will please excuse my ignorance, I didn't even know his father was still alive. It's a pleasure to meet you." He held out his fleshy palm and pumped Brannon's calloused right hand.

The other reporter walked over to where he

was standing. Have you heard about your son's latest shootout? He backed down a whole gang of fifty up in Utah — "

"And," the other man spoke in a rising fervor, "he gunned down that villainous Trevor in a face-to-face shootout on the streets of Medicine Hat."

Brannon hesitated. "Eh . . . well, I guess I didn't hear about that one."

"Yes, sir, it's true. That's the way it came over the telegraph. 'Course we thought we'd ride out here and get it straight from Stuart Brannon himself. When do you expect him back?"

"Has either of you ever met my . . . eh, Stuart Brannon?"

"No, sir, we haven't."

"Well, when he comes home from Utah, he always comes on that northern road. Now I'm not sayin' you'll meet him, but the odds are a lot better of getting a story up there on the road than hanging around this place."

The shorter of the two pushed back his hat and put his hands on his hips. "I was thinking the same thing myself. Thank your cook for the coffee and hospitality, and we'll just mosey up that northern road."

Littlefoot had turned Six Bits and Dos Vientos into the corrals and jogged over to Brannon as he waved good-bye to the men.

"What did they want?"

"They wanted to talk to you."

"Me?"

"Yeah, they said they wanted to talk to my son."

Señora Pacifica joined them in the yard. "Stuart, was that a very polite way to treat them?"

"Polite? Do I have to be polite to someone who calls you the cook?"

"Cook?"

"Yeah, I figured they got off pretty easy. Now what in the world are you doing here? Didn't Tap send you the telegram?"

"Mr. Andrews sent the telegram." She glanced at the north road and the departing reporters. "Did you do all those things they mentioned?"

"You know the papers — they always exaggerate. Why did you stay at the ranch? It could have been dangerous."

"Is Trevor dead? I wasn't about to leave, and you knew it."

"Yeah, he's . . . wait a minute! Let's try one conversation at a time. I'll tell you about Trevor later. Why are you here?"

Señora Pacifica pointed at the wagon. "Tell me about Elizabeth first."

"Oh . . . yeah . . . eh, Littlefoot, how about you throwing a couple shovels out of the barn into the wagon? Then leave that team hitched. But make sure they get some water and oats."

The boy ran toward the barn.

"Did you get to Elizabeth before . . ."

"Yeah." Brannon pried his eyes from the Señora and looked up at the piñon pines on the hill. "She died in my arms." He could feel her hand slip into his. They strolled toward the fruit trees away from Littlefoot.

"Did she tell him the truth about his real father."

"Yep."

"How did he take it?"

"About like I would have at that age," Brannon admitted.

"So what happens now?"

"I promised her I'd raise the boy. He's a good kid, Vickie. And he's a stander. He's already stuck by me more than once."

"I am happy for you, Stuart Brannon."

He glanced over to see a tear slip down her cheek.

"Did I say something wrong . . . are you all right?"

"Yes, I am fine, thank you. I cry for happiness. You have been a lonely man for a long time. It will be good for you to have another to look after. It is like an answer to prayers."

"Well, I'm not sure what I'm getting into. But it does make that hard winter at Broken Arrow Crossing seem to have more purpose. But back to the telegram. Didn't I make it clear what I wanted?"

"Oh, yes." She pulled the folded telegram out of her sleeve, brushed back her long black hair, and began to read: " 'Dearest Victoria, please return to the hacienda immediately. Your life could be in danger. With all my deepest love and most ardent affection, Stuart Brannon.' "

" 'Dearest'?" Brannon choked, " 'Deepest? Ardent?' "

"Yes," she said smiling, "it was so sweet of you!"

"But I didn't . . ."

"Of course you didn't! So I waited to find out who was sending out telegrams over your name!"

"But . . . but the rest was true. You could have been in danger!"

"Stuart, did you think I'm going to run home and sit in my house in the Sierra Madres for six months wondering whatever happened to that Brannon fellow? I needed to know your condition."

"Well," Brannon said with a grin, "what is my condition?"

"Your arm is ripped up. A new shirt ruined. You are limping, covered with dirt, and you are about to go up on that hill and bury another woman whom you were fond of. I'd say it's the same old Stuart Brannon. But yours was not the only telegram I received."

"Who else sent you one?"

"Ramon. He says the government is threatening to take away the mountain pasture land, and I am needed in Monterrey. He asked if the Señora is planning on returning to her hacienda, or does she intend to ride off with some Arizona cowboy."

Brannon looked her in the eyes. "What is the Señora's answer?"

"With regrets . . . I will go home to face the lions in Monterrey," she sighed.

"But you will stay until tomorrow?"

"Certainly."

"I want to come down to the hacienda after the spring work. I've told Littlefoot all about it."

"You know you are always welcome."

"That's the good part, isn't it, Vickie? Knowing that there is another place on this earth where you are always welcome."

"Yes," she agreed, "that seems to be our special gift for one another, Mr. Brannon."

"Will you come up to the piñons for the burial?"

"I mean no disrespect," she replied, "but I believe this is a time for you and Littlefoot. I will play the cook. I will prepare some supper."

"The cook! If those two show up talking like that again, I'll stuff them in the outhouse and lock the door!"

"Speaking of which," the Señora continued, "how did that door get so shot up?"

"I don't want to talk about it."

The sun had sunk low on the western horizon by the time they finished digging. According to Littlefoot's wishes, they dug the grave a few feet away from Lisa Brannon's. It had been a slow, tedious, rocky task. Brannon's throbbing right arm slowed progress.

Carefully they eased the oak coffin out of the wagon and scooted it over by the open hole. Using ropes that Brannon had brought for the purpose, they lowered the box to the bottom of the grave and very carefully began to fill the dirt in around it, stopping to tamp down every foot or so of soil.

Finally, in the declining minutes of daylight they pounded flat the last clods on top of the mound.

"I will buy a marble stone like these others next time we're in Prescott," Brannon offered.

"Yes. I know what I want it to read," Littlefoot said.

"What's that?"

"I want it to say, 'This is Elizabeth. She was a very good mother.' "

"Sounds fine to me. Do you mind if I put the date of her birth and her death?"

"Do you know when she was born? She never told me."

Brannon tossed the shovels back into the wagon. "We'll just take a guess. Now we ought to have a little reading." He pulled his black Bible from the wagon and walked over to the grave.

He squinted his eyes and pointed the pages toward the waning sunlight. He read Psalm 23, 90, and 121, sections about Heaven from Revelation 21 and 22, and several verses about the resurrection of believers from 1 Corinthians 15. Then he pulled off his hat and bowed his head.

"Lord, this isn't the first time I've had to bury a lady on this mountain. Now You know Elizabeth was a good mother and a fine lady. She deserves the rest she's getting in Heaven, but me and Littlefoot . . . well, we'll miss her. So we release her into Your hands. Help us not to be too lonely, and help us always to have fond memories of her. 'O Lamb of God who taketh away the sins of the world, have mercy upon us. O Lamb of God who taketh away the sins of the world, grant us Thy peace.' Amen."

Littlefoot jammed his hat back on his head and reached over and pulled Brannon's left arm around his shoulder. With his one good arm, he held the boy tight.

They stood there in silence until the first star appeared in the darkening sky.

Lisa, this is Elizabeth. We've talked about her before. I just didn't know she'd be going to live with you all so soon. Now she doesn't know anybody much up there, so I would appreciate it if you would sort of introduce her around. She can be a little bashful with strangers . . . not like you at all, so maybe if you could check in on her from time to time . . . and she'll miss her boy . . . I don't know how things work up there, but maybe you could let her visit with our boy some. And tell her I'll take good care of hers.

Littlefoot tugged on Brannon's sleeve.

"It is getting quite dark . . . this day is over."

"Yeah," Brannon sighed. "Maybe you're right, son. One day's ending, and a new one begins. Let's go home and get ready for tomorrow."